Murder is Easy

Agatha Christie was born in Torquay and encouraged to write by
Eden Phillpotts, the Devon playwright. In her first book, *The
Mysterious Affair at Styles*, she created the now famous Belgian
detective, Hercule Poirot, who is as popular as Conan Doyle's
Sherlock Holmes. This was published in 1920, and her
acknowledged masterpiece, *The Murder of Roger Ackroyd*, was
published in 1926. She wrote over seventy-five detective novels,
romantic novels under the pseudonym of Mary Westmacott, and
many short stories and plays – including *The Mousetrap,* which is
still running after more than twenty years. MGM have filmed many
of her stories including *Ten Little Niggers, Witness for the
Prosecution* and *Murder on the Orient Express*. Hercule Poirot finally
died in *Curtain* which, although written twenty years earlier, was
published just before Agatha Christie's death in 1976. She was
married to Sir Max Mallowan, the well-known archaeologist, and
was a Commander of the Order of the British Empire.

Agatha Christie
Murder is easy

Pan Books London and Sydney

First published 1939 by William Collins Sons and Co Ltd
This edition published 1951 by Pan Books Ltd,
Cavaye Place, London SW10 9PG
2nd printing (reset) 1951
9th printing 1977
Copyright Agatha Christie Mallowan 1938, 1939
ISBN 0 330 23779 9
Printed in Great Britain by
Cox & Wyman Ltd, London, Reading and Fakenham

Dedicated to

ROSALIND and SUSAN
The First Two Critics of this Book

CHAPTER ONE

A Fellow-Traveller

ENGLAND!

England after many years!

How was he going to like it?

Luke Fitzwilliam asked himself that question as he walked down the gang-plank to the dock. It was present at the back of his mind all through the wait in the Customs' shed. It came suddenly to the fore when he was finally seated in the boat-train.

England on leave was one thing. Plenty of money to blue (to begin with anyway!), old friends to look up, meetings with other fellows home like himself—a carefree atmosphere of " Well, it won't be long. Might as well enjoy myself! Soon be going back."

But now there was no question of going back. No more of the hot stifling nights, no more blinding sun and tropical beauty of rich vegetation, no more lonely evenings reading and re-reading old copies of *The Times*.

Here he was, honourably retired on a pension, with some small private means of his own, a gentleman of leisure, come home to England. What was he going to do with himself?

England! England on a June day, with a grey sky and a sharp biting wind. Nothing welcoming about her on a day like this! And the people! Heavens, the people! Crowds of them, all with grey faces like the sky—anxious worried faces. The houses, too, springing up everywhere like mushrooms. Nasty little houses! Revolting little houses! Chicken coops in the grandiose manner all over the countryside!

With an effort Luke Fitzwilliam averted his eyes from the landscape outside the railway carriage window and settled down to a perusal of the papers he had just bought. *The Times,* the *Daily Clarion* and *Punch*.

He started with the *Daily Clarion*. The *Clarion* was given over entirely to Epsom.

7

Luke thought: "A pity we didn't get in yesterday. Haven't seen the Derby run since I was nineteen."

He had drawn a horse in the Club sweep and he looked now to see what the *Clarion's* racing correspondent thought of its chance. He found it dismissed contemptuously in a sentence. "*Of the others, Jujube the II., Mark's Mile, Santony and Jerry Boy are hardly likely to qualify for a place. A likely outsider is——*"

But Luke paid no attention to the likely outsider. His eye had shifted to the betting. Jujube the II. was listed at a modest 40 to 1.

He glanced at his watch. A quarter to four. "Well," he thought. "It's over now." And he wished he'd had a bet on Clarigold who was the second favourite.

Then he opened *The Times* and became absorbed in more serious matters.

Not for long, however, for a fierce looking colonel in the corner opposite was so incensed at what he himself had just read that he had to pass on his indignation to his fellow-passenger. A full half-hour passed before the colonel tired of saying what he thought about "these damned Communist agitators, sir."

The colonel died down at last and finally dropped off to sleep with his mouth open. Shortly afterwards the train slowed down and finally stopped. Luke looked out of the window. They were in a large empty-looking station with many platforms. He caught sight of a bookstall some way up the platform with a placard: DERBY RESULT. Luke opened the door, jumped out, and ran towards the bookstall. A moment later he was staring with a broad grin at a few smudged lines in the stop press.

Derby Result
JUJUBE THE II.
MAZEPPA
CLARIGOLD

Luke grinned broadly. A hundred pounds to blue! Good old Jujube the II., so scornfully dismissed by all the tipsters. He folded the paper, still grinning to himself, and turned back—to face emptiness. In the excitement of Jujube the II.'s victory, his train had slipped out of the station unnoticed by him.

"When the devil did that train go out?" he demanded of a gloomy-looking porter.

The latter replied:

"What train? There hasn't been no train since the 3.14."

"There was a train here just now. I got out of it. The boat express."

The porter replied austerely:

"The boat express don't stop anywhere till London."

"But it did," Luke assured him. "I got out of it."

"No stop anywhere till London," repeated the porter immovably.

"It stopped at this very platform and I got out of it, I tell you."

Faced by facts, the porter changed his ground.

"You didn't ought to have done," he said reproachfully. "It don't stop here."

"But it did."

"That 'twas signal, that was. Signal against it. It didn't what you'd call ' stop.' "

"I'm not so good at these fine distinctions as you are," said Luke. "The point is, what do I do next?"

The porter, a man of slow ideas, repeated reproachfully: "You didn't ought to have got out."

"We'll admit that," said Luke. "The wrong is done, past all recall—weep we never so bitterly we can never bring back the dead past—Quoth the raven ' Nevermore '—The moving finger writes; and having writ moves on, etc., etc., and so on and so forth. What I'm trying to get at is, what do you, a man experienced in the service of the railway company, advise me to do now?"

"You're asking what you'd better do?"

"That," said Luke, "is the idea. There are, I presume, trains that stop, really officially stop, here?"

"Reckon," said the porter. "You'd best go on by the 4.25."

"If the 4.25 goes to London," said Luke, "the 4.25 is the train for me."

Reassured on that point, Luke strolled up and down the platform. A large board informed him that he was at Fenny Clayton Junction for Wychwood-under-Ashe, and presently a train consisting of one carriage pushed backwards by an antiquated little engine came slowly puffing in and deposited itself in a modest bay. Six or seven people alighted, and crossing over a bridge, came to join Luke on his platform. The gloomy porter suddenly awoke to life and began pushing about a large truck of crates and baskets, another porter joined him and began to rattle milk cans. Fenny Clayton awoke to life.

At last, with immense importance the London train came in. The third-class carriages were crowded, and of firsts there were only three and each one contained a traveller or travellers. Luke scrutinised each compartment. The first, a smoker, contained a gentleman of military aspect smoking a cigar. Luke felt he had had enough of Anglo-Indian colonels to-day. He passed on to the next one, which contained a tired-looking genteel young woman, possibly a nursery governess, and an active-looking small boy of about three. Luke passed on quickly. The next door was open and the carriage contained one passenger, an elderly lady. She reminded Luke slightly of one of his aunts, his Aunt Mildred, who had courageously allowed him to keep a grass snake when he was ten years old. Aunt Mildred had been decidedly a good aunt as aunts go. Luke entered the carriage and sat down.

After some five minutes of intense activity on the part of milk vans, luggage trucks and other excitements, the train moved slowly out of the station. Luke unfolded his paper and turned to such items of news as might interest a man who had already read his morning paper.

He did not hope to read it for long. Being a man of many aunts, he was fairly certain that the nice old lady in the corner did not propose to travel in silence to London.

He was right—a window that needed adjusting, a dropped umbrella—and the old lady was telling him what a good train this was.

" Only an hour and ten minutes. That's very good, you know, very good indeed. Much better than the morning one. That takes an hour and forty minutes."

She went on:

" Of course, nearly every one goes by the morning one. I mean, when it is the cheap day it's silly to go up in the afternoon. I meant to go up this morning, but Wonky Pooh was missing—that's my cat, a Persian, such a beauty only he's had a painful ear lately—and of course I couldn't leave home till he was found ! "

Luke murmured:

" Of course not," and let his eyes drop ostentatiously to his paper. But it was of no avail. The flood went on.

" So I just made the best of a bad job and took the afternoon train instead, and of course it's a blessing in one way because it's not so crowded—not that that matters when one is travelling first class. Of course, I don't usually do that. I mean, I should consider it an *extravagance,* what with taxes and one's dividends being less and servants' wages so much more and everything—but really I was so upset—because, you see, I'm going up on very important business, and I wanted to think out exactly what I was going to say—just quietly, you know——" Luke repressed a smile. " And when there are people you know travelling up too—well, one can't be un- friendly—so I thought just for once, the expense was *quite permissible*—though I do think nowadays there is so much waste—and nobody saves or thinks of the future. One is sorry the seconds were ever abolished—it did make just that little difference.

" Of course," she went on quickly, with a swift glance at Luke's bronzed face, " I know soldiers on leave have to travel first class. I mean, being officers, it's expected of them——"

Luke sustained the inquisitive glance of a pair of bright twinkling eyes. He capitulated at once. It would come to it, he knew, in the end.

" I'm not a soldier," he said.

" Oh, I'm sorry. I didn't mean—I just thought—you were so brown—perhaps home from the East on leave."

" I'm home from the East," said Luke. " But not on leave." He stalled off further researches with a bald statement. " I'm a policeman."

" In the police? Now really, that's very interesting. A

dear friend of mine—*her* boy has just joined the Palestine police."

"Mayang Straits," said Luke, taking another short cut.

"Oh, dear—very interesting. Really, it's quite a coincidence —I mean, that you should be travelling in this carriage. Because, you see, this business I'm going up to town about—well, actually it is to Scotland Yard I'm going."

"Really?" said Luke.

He thought to himself, "Will she run down soon like a clock or will this go on all the way to London?" But he did not really mind very much, because he had been very fond of his Aunt Mildred, and he remembered how she had once stumped up a fiver in the nick of time. Besides, there was something very cosy and English about old ladies like this old lady and his Aunt Mildred. There was nothing at all like them in the Mayang Straits. They could be classed with plum pudding on Christmas Day and village cricket and open fireplaces with wood fires. The sort of things you appreciated a good deal when you hadn't got them and were on the other side of the world. (They were also the sort of thing you got very bored with when you had a good deal of them, but as has been already told, Luke had only landed in England three or four hours ago.)

The old lady was continuing happily:

"Yes, I meant to go up this morning—and then, as I told you, I was so worried about Wonky Pooh. But you don't think it will be too late, do you? I mean, there aren't any special office hours at Scotland Yard."

"I don't think they close down at four or anything like that," said Luke.

"No, of course, they couldn't, could they? I mean, somebody might want to report a serious crime at any minute, mightn't they?"

"Exactly," said Luke.

For a moment the old lady relapsed into silence. She looked worried.

"I always think it's better to go right to the fountainhead," she said at last. "John Reed is quite a nice fellow— that's our constable in Wychwood—a very civil-spoken, pleasant man—but I don't feel, you know—that he would be quite the person to deal with anything serious. He's quite used to dealing with people who've drunk too much, or with exceeding the speed limit, or lighting-up time—or people who haven't taken out a dog licence—and perhaps with burglary even. But I don't think—I'm quite sure—he isn't the person to deal with *murder*!"

Luke's eyebrows rose.

" Murder?"

The old lady nodded vigorously.

" Yes, murder. You're surprised, I can see. I was myself at first. . . . I really couldn't believe it. I thought I must be imagining things."

" Are you quite sure you weren't?" Luke asked gently.

" Oh, no." She shook her head positively. " I might have been the first time, but not the second, or the third or the fourth. After that one *knows*."

Luke said:

" Do you mean there have been—er—several murders?"

The quiet gentle voice replied:

" A good many, I'm afraid."

She went on:

" That's why I thought it would be best to go straight to Scotland Yard and tell them about it. Don't *you* think that's the best thing to do?"

Luke looked at her thoughtfully, then he said:

" Why, yes—I think you're quite right."

He thought to himself:

" They'll know how to deal with her. Probably get half a dozen old ladies a week coming in burbling about the amount of murders committed in their nice quiet country villages! There may be a special department for dealing with the old dears."

And he saw in imagination a fatherly superintendent, or a good-looking young inspector, tactfully murmuring:

" Thank you, ma'am, very grateful to you, I'm sure. Now just go back and leave it all in our hands and don't worry any more about it."

He smiled a little to himself at the picture. He thought:

" I wonder why they get these fancies? Deadly dull lives, I suppose—an unacknowledged craving for drama. Some old ladies, so I've heard, fancy every one is poisoning their food."

He was roused from these meditations by the thin, gentle voice continuing:

"You know, I remember reading once—I think it was the Abercrombie case—of course *he'd* poisoned quite a lot of people before any suspicion was aroused—what was I saying? Oh, yes, somebody said that there was a look—a special look that he gave any one—and then very shortly afterwards that person would be taken ill. I didn't really believe that when I read about it—but it's true!"

"What's true?"

"The look on a person's face . . ."

Luke stared at her. She was trembling a little, and her nice pink cheeks had lost some of their colour.

"I saw it first with Amy Gibbs—and *she* died. And then it was Carter. And Tommy Pierce. But now—yesterday— it was Dr. Humbleby—and he's such a *good* man—a *really* good man. Carter, of course, drank, and Tommy Pierce was a dreadfully cheeky impertinent little boy, and bullied the tiny boys, twisting their arms and pinching them. I didn't feel quite so badly about them, but Dr. Humbleby's different. He *must* be saved. And the terrible thing is that if I went to him and told him about it he wouldn't believe me! He'd only laugh! And John Reed wouldn't believe me either. But at Scotland Yard it will be different. Because, naturally, they're *used* to crime there!"

She glanced out of the window.

"Oh, dear, we shall be in in a minute." She fussed a little, opening and shutting her bag, collecting her umbrella.

"Thank you—thank you so much." This to Luke as he picked the umbrella up for the second time. "It's been such a *relief* talking to you—most kind of you, I'm sure—so glad you think I'm doing the right thing."

Luke said kindly:

"I'm sure they'll give you good advice at Scotland Yard."

"I really am most grateful." She fumbled in her bag. "My card—oh, dear, I only have one—I must keep that— for Scotland Yard——"

"Of course, of course——"

"But my name is Pinkerton."

"Very suitable name, too, Miss Pinkerton," said Luke, smiling, adding hastily as she looked a little bewildered, "My name is Luke Fitzwilliam."

As the train drew in to the platform he added:

"Can I get you a taxi?"

"Oh, no, thank you." Miss Pinkerton seemed quite shocked at the idea. "I shall take the tube. That will take me to Trafalgar Square, and I shall walk down Whitehall."

"Well, good luck," said Luke.

Miss Pinkerton shook him warmly by the hand.

"So kind," she murmured again. "You know, just at first I thought you didn't believe me."

Luke had the grace to blush.

"Well," he said. "So many murders! Rather hard to do a lot of murders and get away with it, eh?"

Miss Pinkerton shook her head.

She said earnestly:

"No, no, my dear boy, *that's* where you're wrong. It's very easy to kill—so long as no one suspects you. And you see, the person in question is just the last person any one *would* suspect!"

"Well, anyway, good luck," said Luke.

Miss Pinkerton was swallowed up in the crowd. He himself went off in search of his luggage, thinking as he did so:

"Just a little bit batty? No, I don't think so. A vivid imagination, that's all. Hope they let her down lightly. Rather an old dear."

CHAPTER TWO

Obituary Notice

JIMMY LORRIMER was one of Luke's oldest friends. As a matter of course, Luke stayed with Jimmy as soon as he got to London. It was with Jimmy that he sallied forth on the evening of his arrival in search of amusement. It was Jimmy's coffee that he drank with an aching head the morning after, and it was Jimmy's voice that went unanswered while he read twice over a small insignificant paragraph in the morning paper.

"Sorry, Jimmy," he said, coming to himself with a start.

"What were you absorbed in—the political situation?"

Luke grinned.

"No fear. No, it's rather queer—old pussy I travelled up with in the train yesterday got run over."

"Probably trusted to a Belisha Beacon," said Jimmy. "How do you know it's her?"

"Of course, it mayn't be. But it's the same name—Pinkerton—she was knocked down and killed by a car as she was crossing Whitehall. The car didn't stop."

"Nasty business," said Jimmy.

"Yes, poor old bean. I'm sorry. She reminded me of my Aunt Mildred."

"Whoever was driving that car will be for it. Bring it in manslaughter as likely as not. I tell you, I'm scared stiff of driving a car nowadays."

"What have you got at present in the way of a car?"

"Ford V 8. I tell you, my boy——"

The conversation became severely mechanical.

Jimmy broke it off to ask:

"What the devil are you humming?"

Luke was humming to himself:

"*Fiddle de dee, fiddle de dee, the fly has married the humble bee.*"

He apologised.

"Nursery rhyme remembered from my childhood. Can't think what put it into my head."

It was over a week later that Luke, carelessly scanning the front page of *The Times,* gave a sudden startled exclamation.

"Well, I'm damned!"

Jimmy Lorrimer looked up.

"What's the matter?"

Luke did not answer. He was staring at a name in the printed column.

Jimmy repeated his question.

Luke raised his head and looked at his friend. His expression was so peculiar that Jimmy was quite taken aback.

" What's up, Luke? You look as though you'd seen a ghost."

For a minute or two the other did not reply. He dropped the paper, strode to the window and back again. Jimmy watched him with increasing surprise.

Luke dropped into a chair and leaned forward.

" Jimmy, old son, do you remember my mentioning an old lady I travelled up to town with—the day I arrived in England?"

" The one you said reminded you of your Aunt Mildred? And then she got run over by a car?"

" That's the one. Listen, Jimmy. The old girl came out with a long rigmarole of how she was going up to Scotland Yard to tell them about a lot of murders. There was a murderer loose in her village—that's what it amounted to, and he's been doing some pretty rapid execution."

" You didn't tell me she was batty," said Jimmy.

" I didn't think she was."

" Oh, come now, old boy, wholesale murder——"

Luke said impatiently:

" I didn't think she was off her head. I thought she was just letting her imagination run away with her like old ladies sometimes do."

" Well, yes, I suppose that might have been it. But she probably was a bit touched as well, I should think."

" Never mind what *you* think, Jimmy. At the moment, *I'm* telling *you*, see?"

" Oh, quite—quite—get on with it."

" She was quite circumstantial, mentioned one or two victims by name and then explained that what had really rattled her was the fact that she knew who the next victim was going to be."

" Yes?" said Jimmy encouragingly.

" Sometimes a name sticks in your head for some silly reason or other. This name stuck in mine because I linked it up with a silly nursery rhyme they used to sing to me when I was a kid. *Fiddle de dee, fiddle de dee, the fly has married the humble bee.*"

" Very intellectual, I'm sure, but what's the point?"

" The point, my good ass, is that the man's name was

Humbleby—Dr. Humbleby. My old lady said Dr. Humbleby would be the next, and she was distressed because he was 'such a good man.' The name stuck in my head because of the aforementioned rhyme."

"Well?" said Jimmy.

"Well, look at this."

Luke passed over the paper, his finger pressed against an entry in the column of deaths.

HUMBLEBY.—On June 13, suddenly, at his residence, Sandgate, Wychwood-under-Ashe, JOHN EDWARD HUMBLEBY, M.D., beloved husband of JESSIE ROSE HUMBLEBY. Funeral Friday. No flowers, by request.

"You see, Jimmy? That's the name and the place and he's a doctor. What do you make of it?"

Jimmy took a moment or two to answer. His voice was serious when he said at last rather uncertainly:

"I suppose it's just a damned odd coincidence."

"Is it, Jimmy? Is it? Is that all it is?"

Luke began to walk up and down again.

"What else could it be?" asked Jimmy.

Luke wheeled round suddenly.

"Suppose that every word that dear bleating old sheep said was *true*! Suppose that that fantastic story was just the plain literal truth!"

"Oh, come now, old boy! That would be a bit thick! Things like that don't happen."

"What about the Abercrombie case? Wasn't he supposed to have done away with a goodish few?"

"More than ever came out," said Jimmy. "A pal of mine had a cousin who was the local coroner. I heard a bit through him. They got Abercrombie for feeding the local vet with arsenic, then they dug up his wife and she was full of it, and it's pretty certain his brother-in-law went the same way—and that wasn't all, by a long chalk. This pal of mine told me the unofficial view was that Abercrombie had done away with at least fifteen people in his time. *Fifteen!*"

"Exactly. So these things *do* happen!"

" Yes, but they don't happen often."

" How do you know? They may happen a good deal oftener than you suppose."

" There speaks the police wallah! Can't you forget you're a policeman now that you've retired into private life?"

" Once a policeman, always a policeman, I suppose," said Luke. " Now look here, Jimmy, supposing that before Abercrombie had got so foolhardy as fairly to push his murders under the noses of the police, some dear loquacious old spinster had just simply guessed what he was up to and had trotted off to tell some one in authority all about it. Do you suppose they'd have listened to her?"

Jimmy grinned.

" No fear!"

" Exactly. They'd have said she'd got bats in the belfry. Just as *you* said! Or they'd have said, ' Too much imagination. Not enough to do.' As *I* said! *And both of us, Jimmy, would have been wrong.*"

Lorrimer took a moment or two to consider, then he said:

" What's the position exactly—as it appears to you?"

Luke said slowly:

" The case stands like this. I was told a story—an improbable, but not an impossible story. One piece of evidence, the death of Dr. Humbleby, supports that story. And there's one other significant fact. Miss Pinkerton was going to Scotland Yard with this improbable story of hers. *But she didn't get there.* She was run over and killed by a car that didn't stop."

Jimmy objected.

" You don't know that she didn't get there. She might have been killed after her visit, not before."

" She might have been, yes—but I don't think she was."

" That's pure supposition. It boils down to this—you believe in this—this melodrama."

Luke shook his head sharply.

" No, I don't say that. All I say is, there's a case for investigation."

" In other words, *you* are going to Scotland Yard?"

" No, it hasn't come to that yet—not nearly. As you say, this man Humbleby's death may be merely a coincidence."

" Then what, may I ask, is the idea?"

" The idea is to go down to this place and look into the matter."

" So that's the idea, is it?"

" Don't you agree that that is the only sensible way to set about it?"

Jimmy stared at him, then he said:

" Are you *serious* about this business, Luke?"

" Absolutely."

" Suppose the whole thing's a mare's nest?"

" That would be the best thing that could happen."

" Yes, of course . . ." Jimmy frowned. " But you don't think it is, do you?"

" My dear fellow, I'm keeping an open mind." Jimmy was silent for a minute or two. Then he said:

" Got any plan? I mean, you'll have to have some *reason* for suddenly arriving in this place."

" Yes, I suppose I shall."

" No 'suppose' about it. Do you realise what a small English country town is like? Any one new sticks out a mile!"

" I shall have to adopt a disguise," said Luke with a sudden grin. " What do you suggest? Artist? Hardly—I can't draw, let alone paint."

" You could be a modern artist," suggested Jimmy. " Then that wouldn't matter."

But Luke was intent on the matter in hand.

" An author? Do authors go to strange country inns to write? They might, I suppose. A fisherman, perhaps—but I'll have to find out if there's a handy river. An invalid ordered country air? I don't look the part, and anyway every one goes to a nursing home nowadays. I might be looking for a house in the neighbourhood. But that's not very good. Hang it all, Jimmy, there must be *some* plausible reason for a hearty stranger to descend upon an English village?"

Jimmy said:

" Wait a sec—give me that paper again."

Taking it, he gave it a cursory glance and announced triumphantly:

" I thought so! Luke, old boy—to put it in a nutshell—
I'll fix you O.K. Everything's as easy as winking!"

Luke wheeled round.

" What?"

Jimmy was continuing with modest pride:

" I thought something struck a chord! Wychwood-under-
Ashe. Of course! The very place!"

" Have you, by any chance, a pal who knows the coroner
there?"

" Not this time. Better than that, my boy. Nature, as you
know, has endowed me plentifully with aunts and cousins—
my father having been one of a family of thirteen. Now
listen to this: *I have a cousin in Wychwood-under-Ashe.*"

" Jimmy, you're a blinking marvel."

" It is pretty good, isn't it?" said Jimmy modestly.

" Tell me about him?"

" It's a her. Her name's Bridget Conway. For the last two
years she's been secretary to Lord Whitfield."

" The man who owns those nasty little weekly papers?"

" That's right. Rather a nasty little man too! Pompous!
He was born in Wychwood-under-Ashe, and being the kind
of snob who rams his birth and breeding down your throat
and glories in being self-made, he has returned to his home
village, bought up the only big house in the neighbourhood
(it belonged to Bridget's family originally, by the way) and
is busy making the place into a ' model estate.' "

" And your cousin is his secretary?"

" She was," said Jimmy darkly. " Now she's gone one
better! She's engaged to him!"

" Oh," said Luke, rather taken aback.

" He's a catch, of course," said Jimmy. " Rolling in money.
Bridget took rather a toss over some fellow—it pretty well
knocked the romance out of her. I dare say this will pan out
very well. She'll probably be kind of firm with him and he'll
eat out of her hand."

" And where do I come in?"

Jimmy replied promptly.

" You go down there to stay—you'd better be another
cousin. Bridget's got so many that one more or less won't

matter. I'll fix that up with her all right. She and I have always been pals. Now for your reason for going there—witchcraft, my boy."

" Witchcraft?"

" Folklore, local superstitions—all that sort of thing. Wych-wood-under-Ashe has got rather a reputation that way. One of the last places where they had a Witches' Sabbath—witches were still burnt there in the last century—all sorts of traditions. You're writing a book, see? Correlating the customs of the Mayang Straits and old English folklore—points of resem-blance, etc. You know the sort of stuff. Go round with a notebook and interview the oldest inhabitant about local super-stitions and customs. They're quite used to that sort of thing down there, and if you're staying at Ashe Manor it vouches for you."

" What about Lord Whitfield?"

" He'll be all right. He's quite uneducated and completely credulous—actually believes things he reads in his own papers. Anyway Bridget will fix him. Bridget's all right. I'll answer for her."

Luke drew a deep breath.

" Jimmy, old scout, it looks as though the thing is going to be easy. You're a wonder. If you can really fix up with your cousin——"

" That will be absolutely O.K. Leave it to me."

" I'm no end grateful to you."

Jimmy said:

" All I ask is, if you're hunting down a homicidal murderer, let me be in at the death!"

He added sharply:

" What is it?"

Luke said slowly:

" Just something I remembered my old lady saying to me. I'd said to her that it was a bit thick to do a lot of murders and get away with it, and she answered that I was wrong—that it was very easy to kill . . ." He stopped, and then said slowly, " I wonder if that's true, Jimmy? I wonder if it is——"

" What?"

" *Easy to kill . . .*"

CHAPTER THREE

Witch Without Broomstick

THE SUN was shining when Luke came over the hill and down into the little country town of Wychwood-under-Ashe. He had bought a second-hand Standard Swallow, and he stopped for a moment on the brow of the hill and switched off the engine.

The summer day was warm and sunny. Below him was the village, singularly unspoilt by recent developments. It lay innocently and peacefully in the sunlight—mainly composed of a long straggling street that ran along under the overhanging brow of Ashe Ridge.

It seemed singularly remote, strangely untouched. Luke thought, " I'm probably mad. The whole thing's fantastic."

Had he really come here solemnly to hunt down a killer—simply on the strength of some garrulous ramblings on the part of an old lady, and a chance obituary notice?

He shook his head.

"Surely these things don't happen," he murmured. "Or —do they? Luke, my boy, it's up to you to find out if you're the world's most credulous prize ass, or if your policeman's nose has led you hot on the scent."

He switched on the engine, threw in the gear and drove gently down the twisting road and so entered the main street.

Wychwood, as has been said, consists mainly of its one principal street. There were shops, small Georgian houses, prim and aristocratic, with whitened steps and polished knockers, there were picturesque cottages with flower gardens. There was an inn, the Bells and Motley, standing a little back from the street. There was a village green and a duck pond, and presiding over them a dignified Georgian house which Luke thought at first must be his destination, Ashe Manor. But on coming nearer he saw that there was a large painted board announcing that it was the Museum and Library.

Farther on there was an anachronism, a large white modern building, austere and irrelevant to the cheerful haphazardness of the rest of the place. It was, Luke gathered, a local Institute and Lads' Club.

It was at this point that he stopped and asked the way to his destination.

He was told that Ashe Manor was about half a mile farther on—he would see the gates on his right.

Luke continued his course. He found the gates easily—they were of new and elaborate wrought-iron. He drove in, caught a gleam of red brick through the trees, and turned a corner of the drive to be stupefied by the appalling and incongruous castellated mass that greeted his eyes.

While he was contemplating the nightmare, the sun went in. He became suddenly conscious of the overlying menace of Ashe Ridge. There was a sudden sharp gust of wind, blowing back the leaves of the trees, and at that moment a girl came round the corner of the castellated mansion.

Her black hair was blown up off her head by the sudden gust and Luke was reminded of a picture he had once seen—Nevinson's "Witch." The long pale delicate face, the black hair flying up to the stars. He could see this girl on a broomstick flying up to the moon. . . .

She came straight towards him.

"You must be Luke Fitzwilliam. I'm Bridget Conway."

He took the hand she held out. He could see her now as she was—not in a sudden moment of fantasy. Tall, slender, a long delicate face with slightly hollow cheek-bones—ironic black brows—black eyes and hair. She was like a delicate etching, he thought—poignant and beautiful.

He had had an acknowledged picture at the back of his mind during his voyage home to England—a picture of an English girl flushed and sunburnt—stroking a horse's neck, stooping to weed a herbaceous border, sitting holding out her hands to the blaze of a wood fire. It had been a warm gracious vision. . . .

Now—he didn't know if he liked Bridget Conway or not—but he knew that that secret picture wavered and broke up—became meaningless and foolish. . . .

He said:

"How d'you do? I must apologise for wishing myself

on you like this. Jimmy would have it that you wouldn't mind."

"Oh, we don't. We're delighted." She smiled, a sudden curving smile that brought the corners of her long mouth half-way up her cheeks. "Jimmy and I always stand in together. And if you're writing a book on folklore this is a splendid place. All sorts of legends and picturesque spots."

"Splendid," said Luke.

They went together towards the house. Luke stole another glance at it. He discerned now traces of a sober Queen Anne dwelling overlaid and smothered by the florid magnificence. He remembered that Jimmy had mentioned the house as having originally belonged to Bridget's family. That, he thought grimly, was in its unadorned days. Stealing a glance at the line of her profile, at the long beautiful hands, he wondered.

She was about twenty-eight or nine, he supposed. And she had brains. And she was one of those people about whom you knew absolutely nothing unless they chose that you should. . . .

Inside, the house was comfortable and in good taste—the good taste of a first-class decorator. Bridget Conway led the way to a room with bookshelves and comfortable chairs where a tea table stood near the window with two people sitting by it.

She said:

"Gordon, this is Luke, a sort of cousin of a cousin of mine."

Lord Whitfield was a small man with a semi-bald head. His face was round and ingenuous, with a pouting mouth and boiled gooseberry eyes. He was dressed in careless-looking country clothes. They were unkind to his figure, which ran mostly to stomach.

He greeted Luke with affability.

"Glad to see you—very glad. Just come back from the East, I hear? Interesting place. Writing a book, so Bridget tells me. They say too many books are written nowadays. I say no—always room for a good one."

Bridget said, "My aunt, Mrs. Anstruther," and Luke shook hands with a middle-aged woman with a rather foolish mouth.

Mrs. Anstruther, as Luke soon learned, was devoted body

and soul to gardening. She never talked of anything else, and her mind was constantly occupied by considerations of whether some rare plant was likely to do well in the place she intended to put it.

After acknowledging the introduction, she said now:

"You know, Gordon, the ideal spot for a rockery would be just beyond the rose garden, and then you could have the most marvellous water garden where the stream comes through that dip."

Lord Whitfield stretched himself back in his chair.

"You fix all that with Bridget," he said easily. "Rock plants are niggly little things, I think—but that doesn't matter."

Bridget said:

"Rock plants aren't sufficiently in the grand manner for you, Gordon."

She poured out some tea for Luke and Lord Whitfield said placidly:

"That's right. They're not what I call good value for money. Little bits of flowers you can hardly see. . . . I like a nice show in a conservatory, or some good beds of scarlet geraniums."

Mrs. Anstruther, who possessed *par excellence* the gift of continuing with her own subject undisturbed by that of any one else, said:

"I believe those new rock roses would do perfectly in this climate," and proceeded to immerse herself in catalogues.

Throwing his squat little figure back in his chair, Lord Whitfield sipped his tea and studied Luke appraisingly.

"So you write books," he murmured.

Feeling slightly nervous, Luke was about to enter on explanations when he perceived that Lord Whitfield was not really seeking for information.

"I've often thought," said his lordship complacently, "that I'd like to write a book myself."

"Yes?" said Luke.

"I *could*, mark you," said Lord Whitfield. "And a very interesting book it would be. I've come across a lot of interesting people. Trouble is, I haven't got the *time*. I'm a very busy man."

"Of course. You must be."

"You wouldn't believe what I've got on my shoulders,"

said Lord Whitfield. "I take a personal interest in each one of my publications. I consider that I'm responsible for moulding the public mind. Next week millions of people will be thinking and feeling just exactly what I've intended to make them feel and think. That's a very solemn thought. That means responsibility. Well, I don't mind responsibility. I'm not afraid of it. I can *do* with responsibility."

Lord Whitfield swelled out his chest, attempted to draw in his stomach, and glared amiably at Luke.

Bridget Conway said lightly:

"You're a great man, Gordon. Have some more tea."

Lord Whitfield replied simply:

"I *am* a great man. No, I won't have any more tea."

Then, descending from his own Olympian heights to the level of more ordinary mortals, he inquired kindly of his guest:

"Know anybody round this part of the world?"

Luke shook his head. Then, on an impulse, and feeling that the sooner he began to get down to his job the better, he added:

"At least, there's a man here that I promised to look up— friend of friends of mine. Man called Humbleby. He's a doctor."

"Oh!" Lord Whitfield struggled upright in his chair. "Dr. Humbleby? Pity."

"What's a pity?"

"Died about a week ago," said Lord Whitfield.

"Oh, dear," said Luke. "I'm sorry about that."

"Don't think you'd have cared for him," said Lord Whitfield. "Opinionated, pestilential, muddle-headed old fool."

"Which means," put in Bridget, "that he disagreed with Gordon."

"Question of our water supply," said Lord Whitfield. "I may tell you, Mr. Fitzwilliam, that I'm a public spirited man. I've got the welfare of this town at heart. I was born here. Yes, born in this very town———"

With chagrin Luke perceived that they had left the topic of Dr. Humbleby and had reverted to the topic of Lord Whitfield.

"I'm not ashamed of it and I don't care who knows it,"

went on that gentleman. " I had none of your natural advan-
tages. My father kept a boot-shop—yes, a plain boot-shop.
And I served in that shop when I was a young lad. I raised
myself by my own efforts, Fitzwilliam—I determined to get
out of the rut—and I *got* out of the rut! Perseverance, hard
work and the help of God—that's what did it! That's what
made me what I am to-day."

Exhaustive details of Lord Whitfield's career were produced
for Luke's benefit and the former wound up triumphantly :

" And here I am and the whole world's welcome to know
how I've got here! I'm not ashamed of my beginnings—no,
sir—I've come back here where I was born. Do you know what
stands where my father's shop used to be? A fine building
built and endowed by *me*—Institute, Boys' Clubs, everything
tip-top and up to date. Employed the best architect in the
country! I must say he's made a bare plain job of it—looks
like a workhouse or a prison to me—but they say it's all
right, so I suppose it must be."

" Cheer up," said Bridget. " You had your own way over
this house!"

Lord Whitfield chuckled appreciatively.

" Yes, they tried to put it over on me here! Carry out the
original spirit of the building. No, I said, I'm going to *live*
in the place, and I want something to *show* for my money!
When one architect wouldn't do what I wanted I sacked him
and got another. The fellow I got in the end understood
my ideas pretty well."

" He pandered to your worst flights of imagination," said
Bridget.

" She'd have liked the place left as it was," said Lord Whitfield. He patted her arm. " No use living in the past, my dear.
Those old Georges didn't know much. I didn't want a plain
red-brick house. I always had a fancy for a castle—and now
I've got one!" He added, " I know my taste isn't very classy,
so I gave a good firm *carte blanche* to do the inside, and I
must say they haven't done too badly—though some of it is
a bit drab."

" Well," said Luke, a little at a loss for words, " it's a great
thing to know what you want."

" And I usually get it too," said the other, chuckling.

" You nearly didn't get your way about the water scheme," Bridget reminded him.

" Oh, that!" said Lord Whitfield. " Humbleby was a fool. These elderly men are inclined to be pig-headed. They won't listen to reason."

" Dr. Humbleby was rather an outspoken man, wasn't he?" Luke ventured. " He made a good many enemies that way, I should imagine."

" N-no, I don't know that I should say that," demurred Lord Whitfield, rubbing his nose. " Eh, Bridget?"

" He was very popular with every one, I always thought," said Bridget. " I only saw him when he came about my ankle that time, but I thought he was a dear."

" Yes, he was popular enough on the whole," admitted Lord Whitfield. " Though I know one or two people who had it in for him. Pig-headedness again."

" One or two of the people living here?"

Lord Whitfield nodded.

" Lots of little feuds and cliques in a place like this," he said.

" Yes, I suppose so," said Luke. He hesitated, uncertain of his next step.

" What sort of people live here mostly?" he queried.

It was rather a weak question, but he got an instant response.

" Relicts, mostly," said Bridget. " Clergymen's daughters and sisters and wives. Doctors' dittoes. About six women to every man."

" But there are *some* men?" hazarded Luke.

" Oh, yes, there's Mr. Abbot, the solicitor, and young Dr. Thomas, Dr. Humbleby's partner, and Mr. Wake, the rector, and—who else is there, Gordon? Oh! Mr. Ellsworthy, who keeps the antique shop and who is too, too terribly sweet! And Major Horton and his bulldogs."

" There's somebody else I believe my friends mentioned as living down here," said Luke. " They said she was a nice old pussy but talked a lot."

Bridget laughed.

" That applies to half the village!"

" What was the name now? I've got it. Pinkerton."

Lord Whitfield said with a hoarse chuckle:

"Really, you've no luck! She's dead too. Got run over the other day in London. Killed outright."

"You seem to have a lot of deaths here," said Luke lightly. Lord Whitfield bridled immediately.

"Not at all. One of the healthiest places in England. Can't count accidents. They may happen to any one."

But Bridget Conway said thoughtfully:

"As a matter of fact, Gordon, there *have* been a lot of deaths in the last year. They're always having funerals."

"Nonsense, my dear."

Luke said:

"Was Dr. Humbleby's death an accident too?"

Lord Whitfield shook his head.

"Oh, no," he said. "Humbleby died of acute septicæmia. Just like a doctor. Scratched his finger with a rusty nail or something—paid no attention to it, and it turned septic. He was dead in three days."

"Doctors are rather like that," said Bridget. "And of course, they're very liable to infection, I suppose, if they don't take care. It was sad, though. His wife was broken-hearted."

"No good rebelling against the will of providence," said Lord Whitfield easily.

"But was it the will of providence?" Luke asked himself later as he changed into his dinner jacket. Septicæmia? Perhaps. A very sudden death, though.

And there echoed through his head Bridget Conway's lightly spoken words:

"*There have been a lot of deaths in the last year.*"

CHAPTER FOUR

Luke Makes a Beginning

LUKE HAD thought out his plan of campaign with some care, and prepared to put it into action without more ado when he came down to breakfast the following morning.

The gardening aunt was not in evidence, but Lord Whitfield was eating kidneys and drinking coffee, and Bridget Conway had finished her meal and was standing at the window, looking out.

After good-mornings had been exchanged and Luke had sat down with a plentifully heaped plate of eggs and bacon, he began:

"I must get to work," he said. "Difficult thing is to induce people to talk. You know what I mean—not people like you and—er—Bridget." (He remembered just in time not to say Miss Conway.) "You'd *tell* me anything you knew—but the trouble is you wouldn't *know* the things I want to know—that is the local superstitions. You'd hardly believe the amount of superstition that still lingers in out-of-the-way parts of the world. Why, there's a village in Devonshire. The rector had to remove some old granite menhirs that stood by the church because the people persisted in marching round them in some old ritual every time there was a death. Extraordinary how old heathen rites persist."

"Dare say you're right," said Lord Whitfield. "Education, that's what people need. Did I tell you that I'd endowed a very fine library here? Used to be the old manor house—was going for a song—now it's one of the finest libraries——"

Luke firmly quelled the tendency of the conversation to turn in the direction of Lord Whitfield's doings.

"Splendid," he said heartily. "Good work. You've evidently realised the background of old-world ignorance there is here. Of course, from my point of view, that's just what I want. Old customs—old wives' tales—hints of the old rituals such as——"

31

Here followed almost verbatim a page of a work that Luke had read up for the occasion.

"Deaths are the most hopeful line," he ended. "Burial rites and customs always survive longer than any others. Besides, for some reason or other, village people always like talking about deaths."

"They enjoy funerals," agreed Bridget from the window.

"I thought I'd make that my starting-point," went on Luke. "If I can get a list of recent demises in the parish, track down the relatives and get into conversation, I've no doubt I shall soon get a hint of what I'm after. Whom had I better get the data from—the parson?"

"Mr. Wake would probably be very interested," said Bridget. "He's quite an old dear and a bit of an antiquary. He could give you a lot of stuff, I expect."

Luke had a momentary qualm during which he hoped that the clergyman might not be so efficient an antiquary as to expose his own pretensions.

Aloud he said heartily:

"Good. You've no idea, I suppose, of likely people who've died during the last year."

Bridget murmured:

"Let me see. Carter, of course. He was the landlord of the Seven Stars, that nasty little pub down by the river."

"A drunken ruffian," said Lord Whitfield. "One of these socialistic, abusive brutes, a good riddance."

"And Mrs. Rose, the laundress," went on Bridget. "And little Tommy Pierce—he was a nasty little boy if you like. Oh, of course, and that girl Amy what's-her-name."

Her voice changed slightly as she uttered the last name.

"Amy?" said Luke.

"Amy Gibbs. She was housemaid here and then she went to Miss Waynflete. There was an inquest on her."

"Why?"

"Fool of a girl mixed up some bottles in the dark," said Lord Whitfield.

"She took what she thought was cough mixture and it was hat paint," explained Bridget.

Luke raised his eyebrows.

"Somewhat of a tragedy."

Bridget said:

"There was some idea of her having done it on purpose. Some row with a young man."

She spoke slowly—almost reluctantly.

There was a pause. Luke felt instinctively the presence of some unspoken feeling weighing down the atmosphere.

He thought:

"Amy Gibbs? Yes, that was one of the names old Miss Pinkerton mentioned."

She had also mentioned a small boy—Tommy some one— of whom she had evidently held a low opinion (this, it seemed, was shared by Bridget!) And yes—he was almost sure—the name Carter had been spoken too.

Rising, he said lightly:

"Talking like this makes me feel rather ghoulish—as though I dabbled only in graveyards. Marriage customs are interesting too—but rather more difficult to introduce into conversation unconcernedly."

"I should imagine that was likely," said Bridget with a faint twitch of the lips.

"Ill-wishing or overlooking, there's another interesting subject," went on Luke with a would-be show of enthusiasm. "You often get that in these old-world places. Know of any gossip of that kind here?"

Lord Whitfield slowly shook his head. Bridget Conway said:

"We shouldn't be likely to hear of things like that——"

Luke took it up almost before she finished speaking.

"No doubt about it, I've got to move in lower social spheres to get what I want. I'll be off to the vicarage first and see what I can get there. After that perhaps a visit to the—Seven Stars, did you say? And what about the small boy of unpleasant habits? Did he leave any sorrowing relatives?"

"Mrs. Pierce keeps a tobacco and paper shop in High Street."

"That," said Luke, " is nothing less than providential. Well, I'll be on my way."

With a swift graceful movement Bridget moved from the window.

"I think," she said, "I'll come with you, if you don't mind."

"Of course not."

He said it as heartily as possible, but he wondered if she had noticed that, just for a moment, he had been taken aback.

It would have been easier for him to handle an elderly antiquarian clergyman without an alert discerning intelligence by his side.

"Oh, well," he thought to himself. "It's up to me to do my stuff convincingly."

Bridget said:

"Will you just wait, Luke, while I change my shoes?"

Luke—the Christian name, uttered so easily, gave him a queer warm feeling. And yet what else could she have called him? Since she had agreed to Jimmy's scheme of cousinship she could hardly call him Mr. Fitzwilliam. He thought suddenly and uneasily, "What does she think of it all? In God's name what does she think?"

Queer that that had not worried him beforehand. Jimmy's cousin had just been a convenient abstraction—a lay figure. He had hardly visualised her, just accepted his friend's dictum that "Bridget would be all right."

He had thought of her—if he had thought of her at all— as a little blonde secretary person—astute enough to have captured a rich man's fancy.

Instead she had force, brains, a cool clear intelligence and he had no idea what she was thinking of him. He thought: *She's not an easy person to deceive.*

"I'm ready now."

She had joined him so silently that he had not heard her approach. She wore no hat, and there was no net on her hair. As they stepped out from the house, the wind, sweeping round the corner of the castellated monstrosity, caught her long black hair and whipped it into a sudden frenzy round her face.

She said smiling:

"You need me to show you the way."

"It's very kind of you," he answered punctiliously.

And wondered if he had imagined a sudden swiftly passing ironic smile.

Looking back at the battlements behind him, he said irritably:

" What an abomination! Couldn't any one stop him?"

Bridget answered: " An Englishman's house is his castle
—literally so in Gordon's case! He adores it."

Conscious that the remark was in bad taste, yet unable to
control his tongue, he said:

" It's your old home, isn't it? Do you ' adore ' to see it the
way it is now?"

She looked at him then—a steady slightly amused look it
was.

" I hate to destroy the dramatic picture you are building up,"
she murmured. " But actually I left here when I was two and
a half, so you see the old home motive doesn't apply. I can't
even remember this place."

" You're right," said Luke. " Forgive the lapse into film
language."

She laughed.

" Truth," she said, " is seldom romantic."

And there was a sudden bitter scorn in her voice that startled
him. He flushed a deep red under his tan, then realised suddenly that the bitterness had not been aimed at him. It was
her own scorn and her own bitterness. Luke was wisely silent.
But he wondered a good deal about Bridget Conway. . . .

Five minutes brought them to the church and to the vicarage that adjoined it. They found the vicar in his study.

Alfred Wake was a small stooping old man with very mild
blue eyes, and an absent-minded but courteous air. He seemed
pleased but a little surprised by the visit.

" Mr. Fitzwilliam is staying with us at Ashe Manor," said
Bridget, " and he wants to consult you about a book he is
writing."

Mr. Wake turned his mild inquiring eyes towards the
younger man, and Luke plunged into explanations.

He was nervous—doubly so. Nervous in the first place
because this man had no doubt a far deeper knowledge of
folklore and superstitious rites and customs than one could
acquire by merely hurriedly cramming from a haphazard collection of books. Secondly he was nervous because Bridget
Conway was standing by listening.

Luke was relieved to find that Mr. Wake's special interest
was Roman remains. He confessed gently that he knew very

little of medieval folklore and witchcraft. He mentioned the existence of certain items in the history of Wychwood, offered to take Luke to the particular ledge of hill where it was said the Witches' Sabbaths had been held, but expressed himself regretful that he could add no special information of his own.

Inwardly much relieved, Luke expressed himself as somewhat disappointed, and then plunged into inquiries as to death bed superstitions.

Mr. Wake shook his head gently.

" I am afraid I should be the last person to know about those. My parishioners would be careful to keep anything unorthodox from my ears."

" That's so, of course."

" But I've no doubt, all the same, there *is* a lot of superstition still rife. These village communities are very backward."

Luke plunged boldly.

" I've been asking Miss Conway for a list of all the recent deaths she could remember. I thought I might get at something that way. I suppose you could supply me with a list, so that I could pick out the likelies."

" Yes—yes—that could be managed. Giles, our sexton, a good fellow but sadly deaf, could help you there. Let me see now. There have been a good many—a good many—a treacherous spring and a hard winter behind it—and then a good many accidents—quite a cycle of bad luck there seems to have been."

" Sometimes," said Luke, " a cycle of bad luck is attributed to the presence of a particular person."

" Yes, yes. The old story of Jonah. But I do not think there have been any strangers here—nobody, that is to say, outstanding in any way, and I've certainly never heard any rumour of such feeling—but then again, as I said, perhaps I shouldn't. Now let me see—quite recently we have had Dr. Humbleby and poor Lavinia Pinkerton—a fine man, Dr. Humbleby——"

Bridget put in:

" Mr. Fitzwilliam knows friends of his."

" Do you indeed? Very sad. His loss will be much felt. A man with many friends."

" But surely a man with some enemies too," said Luke. " I'm

only going by what I've heard my friends say," he went on hastily.

Mr. Wake sighed.

"A man who spoke his mind—and a man who wasn't always very tactful, shall we say——" he shook his head. "It does get people's backs up. But he was greatly beloved among the poorer classes."

Luke said carelessly:

"You know I always feel that one of the most unpalatable facts to be faced in life, is the fact that every death that occurs means a gain to some one—I don't mean only financially."

The vicar nodded thoughtfully.

"I see your meaning, yes. We read in an obituary notice that a man is regretted by everybody, but that can only be true very rarely I fear. In Dr. Humbleby's case, there is no denying that his partner, Dr. Thomas, will find his position very much improved by Dr. Humbleby's death."

"How is that?"

"Thomas, I believe, is a very capable fellow—certainly Humbleby always said so, but he didn't get on here very well. He was, I think, over-shadowed by Humbleby who was a man of very definite magnetism. Thomas appeared rather colourless in contrast. He didn't impress his patients at all. I think he worried over it, too, and that made him worse—more nervous and tongue-tied. As a matter of fact I've noticed an astonishing difference already. More aplomb—more personality. I think he feels a new confidence in himself. He and Humbleby didn't always agree, I believe. Thomas was all for newer methods of treatment and Humbleby preferred to stick to the old ways. There were clashes between them more than once—over that as well as over a matter nearer home—but there, I mustn't gossip——"

Bridget said softly and clearly:

"But I think Mr. Fitzwilliam would like you to gossip!"

Luke shot her a quick disturbed look.

Mr. Wake shook his head doubtfully, and then went on, smiling a little in deprecation.

"I am afraid one learns to take too much interest in one's neighbours' affairs. Rose Humbleby is a very pretty girl. One doesn't wonder that Geoffrey Thomas lost his heart. And of

course Humbleby's point of view was quite understandable too
—the girl is young and buried away here she hadn't much
chance of seeing other men."

" He objected?" said Luke.

" Very definitely. Said they were far too young. And of
course young people resent being told that! There was a very
definite coldness between the two men. But I must say that
I'm sure Dr. Thomas was deeply distressed at his partner's
unexpected death."

" Septicæmia, Lord Whitfield told me."

" Yes—just a little scratch that got infected. Doctors run
grave risks in the course of their profession, Mr. Fitzwilliam."

" They do indeed," said Luke.

Mr. Wake gave a sudden start.

" But I have wandered a long way from what we were talking about," he said. " A gossiping old man, I am afraid. We
were speaking of the survival of pagan death customs and of
recent deaths. There was Lavinia Pinkerton—one of our most
kindly Church helpers. Then there was that poor girl, Amy
Gibbs—you might discover something in your line there, Mr.
Fitzwilliam—there was just a suspicion, you know, that it
might have been suicide—and there are certain rather eerie
rites in connection with that type of death. There is an aunt,
not, I fear, a very estimable woman, and not very much
attached to her niece but a great talker."

" Valuable," said Luke.

" Then there was Tommy Pierce—he was in the choir at
one time—a beautiful treble—quite angelic—but not a very
angelic boy otherwise, I am afraid. We had to get rid of him
in the end, he made the other boys behave so badly. Poor
lad, I'm afraid he was not very much liked anywhere. He
was dismissed from the post office where we got him a job
as telegraph boy. He was in Mr. Abbot's office for a while,
but there again he was dismissed very soon—interfered with
some confidential papers, I believe. Then, of course, he was
at Ashe Manor for a time, wasn't he, Miss Conway, as garden
boy, and Lord Whitfield had to discharge him for gross
impertinence. I was so sorry for his mother—a very decent
hard-working soul. Miss Waynflete very kindly got him
some odd window cleaning work. Lord Whitfield objected at

first, then suddenly he gave in—actually it was sad that he did so."

"Why?"

"Because the boy was killed that way. He was cleaning the top windows of the library (the old Hall, you know) and tried some silly fooling—dancing on the window ledge or something of that sort—lost his balance, or else became dizzy, and fell. A nasty business! He never recovered consciousness and died a few hours after they got him to hospital."

"Did any one see him fall?" asked Luke with interest.

"No. He was on the garden side—not the front of the house. They estimate he lay there for about half an hour before any one found him."

"Who did find him?"

"Miss Pinkerton. You remember, the lady I mentioned just now who was unfortunately killed in a street accident the other day. Poor soul, she was terribly upset. A nasty experience! She had obtained permission to take a cutting of some plants and found the boy there lying where he had fallen."

"It must have been a very unpleasant shock," said Luke thoughtfully.

"A greater shock," he thought to himself, "than *you* know . . ."

"A young life cut short is a very sad thing," said the old man shaking his head. "Tommy's faults may have been mainly due to high spirits."

"He was a disgusting bully," said Bridget. "You know he was, Mr. Wake. Always tormenting cats and stray puppies and pinching other little boys."

"I know—I know." Mr. Wake shook his head sadly. "But you know, my dear Miss Conway, sometimes cruelty is not so much innate as due to the fact that imagination is slow in ripening. That is why if you conceive of a grown man with the mentality of a child you realise that the cunning and brutality of a lunatic may be quite unrealised by the man himself. A lack of growth somewhere, that, I am convinced, is at the root of much of the cruelty and stupid brutality in the world to-day. One must put away childish things——"

He shook his head and spread out his hands.

Bridget said in a voice suddenly hoarse:

"Yes, you're right. I know what you mean. A man who is a child is the most frightening thing in the world. . . ."

Luke looked at her with some curiosity. He was convinced that she was thinking of some particular person, and although Lord Whitfield was in some respects exceedingly childish, he did not believe she was thinking of him. Lord Whitfield was slightly ridiculous, but he was certainly not frightening.

Luke Fitzwilliam wondered very much whom the person Bridget was thinking of might be.

CHAPTER FIVE

Visit to Miss Waynflete

MR. WAKE murmured a few more names to himself.

"Let me see now—poor Mrs. Rose, and old Bell and that child of the Elkins and Harry Carter—they're not all my people, you understand. Mrs. Rose and Carter were dissenters. And that cold spell in March took off poor old Ben Stanbury at last—ninety-two he was."

"Amy Gibbs died in April," said Bridget.

"Yes, poor girl—a sad mistake to happen."

Luke looked up to find Bridget watching him. She lowered her eyes quickly. He thought, with some annoyance:

"There's something here that I haven't got on to. Something to do with this girl Amy Gibbs."

When they had taken leave of the vicar and were outside again, he said:

"Just who and what *was* Amy Gibbs?"

Bridget took a minute or two to answer. Then she said —and Luke noticed the slight constraint in her voice:

"Amy was one of the most inefficient housemaids I have ever known."

"That's why she got the sack?"

"No. She stayed out after hours playing about with some young man. Gordon has very moral and old-fashioned views. Sin in his view does not take place until after eleven o'clock, but then it is rampant. So he gave the girl notice and she was impertinent about it!"

Luke asked: "A good-looking girl?"

"Very good-looking."

"She's the one who swallowed hat paint in mistake for cough mixture?"

"Yes."

"Rather a stupid thing to do?" Luke hazarded.

"Very stupid."

"Was she stupid?"

"No, she was quite a sharp girl."

Luke stole a look at her. He was puzzled. Her replies were given in an even tone, without emphasis or even much interest. But behind what she said, there was, he felt convinced, something not put into words.

At that moment Bridget stopped to speak to a tall man who swept off his hat and greeted her with breezy heartiness.

Bridget, after a word or two, introduced Luke.

"This is my cousin, Mr. Fitzwilliam, who is staying at the Manor. He's down here to write a book. This is Mr. Abbot."

Luke looked at Mr. Abbot with some interest. This was the solicitor who had employed Tommy Pierce.

Luke had a somewhat illogical prejudice against lawyers in general—based on the grounds that so many politicians were recruited from their ranks. Also their cautious habit of not committing themselves annoyed him. Mr. Abbot, however, was not at all the conventional type of lawyer, he was neither thin, spare, nor tight-lipped. He was a big florid man, dressed in tweeds with a hearty manner and a jovial effusiveness. There were little creases at the corners of his eyes, and the eyes themselves were more shrewd than one appreciated in a first casual glance.

"Writing a book, eh? Novel?"

"Folklore," said Bridget.

"You've come to the right place for that," said the lawyer. "Wonderfully interesting part of the world here."

"So I've been led to understand," said Luke. "I dare say you could help me a bit. You must come across curious old deeds—or know of some interesting surviving customs."

"Well, I don't know about that—maybe—maybe——"

" Much belief in ghosts round here?" asked Luke.

" As to that I couldn't say—I really couldn't say."

" No haunted houses?"

" No—I don't know of anything of that kind."

" There's the child superstition, of course," said Luke. " Death of a boy child—a violent death that is—the boy always walks. Not a girl child—interesting that."

" Very," said Mr. Abbot. " I never heard that before."

Since Luke had just invented it, that was hardly surprising.

" Seems there's a boy here—Tommy something—was in your office at one time. I've reason to believe they think that *he's* walking."

Mr. Abbot's red face turned slightly purple.

" Tommy Pierce? A good for nothing, prying, meddlesome jackanapes."

" Spirits always seem to be mischievous. Good law-abiding citizens seldom trouble this world after they've left it."

" Who's seen him—what's this story?"

" These things are difficult to pin down," said Luke. " People won't come out into the open with a statement. It's just in the air, so to speak."

" Yes—yes, I suppose so."

Luke changed the subject adroitly.

" The real person to get hold of is the local doctor. They hear a lot in the poorer cases they attend. All sorts of superstitions and charms—probably love philtres and all the rest of it."

" You must get on to Thomas. Good fellow, Thomas, thoroughly up-to-date man. Not like poor old Humbleby."

" Bit of a reactionary, wasn't he?"

" Absolutely pig-headed—a diehard of the worst description."

" You had a real row over the water scheme, didn't you?" asked Bridget.

Again a rich ruddy glow suffused Abbot's face.

" Humbleby stood dead in the way of progress," he said sharply. " He held out against the scheme! He was pretty rude, too, in what he said. Didn't mince his words. Some of the things he said to me were positively actionable."

Bridget murmured: "But lawyers never go to law, do they? They know better."

Abbot laughed immoderately. His anger subsided as quickly as it had arisen.

"Pretty good, Miss Bridget! And you're not far wrong. We who are in it know too much about law, ha, ha. Well, I must be getting along. Give me a call if you think I can help you in any way, Mr.—er——"

"Fitzwilliam," said Luke. "Thanks, I will."

As they walked on Bridget said:

"Your methods, I note, are to make statements and see what they provoke."

"My methods," said Luke, "are not strictly truthful, if that is what you mean?"

"I've noticed that."

A little uneasy, he hesitated what to say next. But before he could speak, she said:

"If you want to hear more about Amy Gibbs, I can take you to some one who could help you."

"Who is that?"

"A Miss Waynflete. Amy went there after she left the Manor. She was there when she died."

"Oh, I see——" he was a little taken aback. "Well—thank you very much."

"She lives just here."

They were crossing the village green. Inclining her head in the direction of the big Georgian house that Luke had noticed the day before, Bridget said: "That's Wych Hall. It's a library now."

Adjoining the Hall was a little house that looked rather like a doll's house in proportion. Its steps were dazzlingly white, its knocker shone and its window curtains showed white and prim.

Bridget pushed open the gate and advanced to the steps. As she did so the front door opened and an elderly woman came out.

She was, Luke thought, completely the country spinster. Her thin form was neatly dressed in a tweed coat and skirt and she wore a grey silk blouse with a cairngorm brooch.

Her hat, a conscientious felt, sat squarely upon her well-shaped head. Her face was pleasant and her eyes, through their pince-nez, decidedly intelligent. She reminded Luke of those nimble black goats that one sees in Greece. Her eyes held just that quality of mild inquiring surprise.

"Good morning, Miss Waynflete," said Bridget. "This is Mr. Fitzwilliam." Luke bowed. "He's writing a book—about deaths and village customs and general gruesomeness."

"Oh, dear," said Miss Waynflete. "How *very* interesting." And she beamed encouragingly upon him.

He was reminded of Miss Pinkerton.

"I thought," said Bridget—and again he noted that curious flat tone in her voice—"that you might tell him something about Amy."

"Oh," said Miss Waynflete. "About Amy? Yes. About Amy Gibbs."

He was conscious of a new factor in her expression. She seemed to be thoughtfully summing him up.

Then, as though coming to a decision, she drew back into the hall.

"Do come in," she said. "I can go out later. No, no," in answer to a protest from Luke. "I had really nothing urgent to do. Just a little unimportant domestic shopping."

The small drawing-room was exquisitely neat and smelled faintly of burnt lavender. There were some Dresden china shepherds and shepherdesses on the mantelpiece, simpering sweetly. There were framed water-colours, two samplers, and three needlework pictures on the wall. There were some photographs of what were obviously nephews and nieces and some good furniture—a Chippendale desk, some little satinwood tables—and a hideous and rather uncomfortable Victorian sofa.

Miss Waynflete offered her guests chairs and then said apologetically:

"I'm afraid I don't smoke myself, so I have no cigarettes, but do please smoke if you like."

Luke refused but Bridget promptly lighted a cigarette.

Sitting bolt upright in a chair with carved arms, Miss Waynflete studied her guest for a moment or two and then, dropping her eyes as though satisfied, she said:

"You want to know about that poor girl Amy? The whole thing was very sad and caused me a great deal of distress. Such a tragic mistake."

"Wasn't there some question of—suicide?" asked Luke. Miss Waynflete shook her head.

"No, no, *that* I cannot believe for a moment. Amy was not at all that type."

"What type was she?" asked Luke bluntly. "I'd like to hear your account of her."

Miss Waynflete said:

"Well, of course, she wasn't at *all* a good servant. But nowadays, really, one is thankful to get *anybody*. She was very slipshod over her work and always wanting to go out— well, of course she was young and girls *are* like that nowadays. They don't seem to realise that their time is their employer's."

Luke looked properly sympathetic and Miss Waynflete proceeded to develop her theme.

"She wasn't the sort of girl I care for—rather a *bold* type —though of course I wouldn't like to say much now that she's dead. One feels un-Christian—though really I don't think that that is a logical reason for suppressing the truth."

Luke nodded. He realised that Miss Waynflete differed from Miss Pinkerton in having a more logical mind and better processes of thought.

"She was fond of admiration," went on Miss Waynflete, "and was inclined to think a lot of herself. Mr. Ellsworthy— he keeps the new antique shop but he is actually a gentleman —he dabbles a little in water-colours and he had done one or two sketches of the girl's head—and I think, you know, that rather gave her *ideas*. She was inclined to quarrel with the young man she was engaged to—Jim Harvey. He's a mechanic at the garage and very fond of her."

Miss Waynflete paused and then went on.

"I shall never forget that dreadful night. Amy had been out of sorts—a nasty cough and one thing and another (those silly cheap silk stockings they will wear and shoes with *paper* soles practically—of course they catch chills) and she'd been to the doctor that afternoon."

Luke asked quickly:

"Dr. Humbleby or Dr. Thomas?"

"Dr. Thomas. And he gave her the bottle of cough mixture that she brought back with her. Something quite harmless, a stock mixture, I believe. She went to bed early and it must have been about one in the morning when the noise began—an awful kind of choking scream. I got up and went to her door but it was locked on the inside. I called to her but couldn't get any answer. Cook was with me and we were both terribly upset. And then we went to the front door and luckily there was Reed (our constable) just passing on his beat, and we called to him. He went round the back of the house and managed to climb up on the outhouse roof, and as her window was open he got in quite easily that way and unlocked the door. Poor girl, it was terrible. They couldn't do anything for her, and she died in Hospital a few hours later."

"And it was—what—hat paint?"

"Yes. Oxalic acid poisoning is what they called it. The bottle was about the same size as the cough linctus one. The latter was on her washstand and the hat paint was by her bed. She must have picked up the wrong bottle and put it by her in the dark ready to take if she felt badly. That was the theory at the inquest."

Miss Waynflete stopped. Her intelligent goat's eyes looked at him, and he was aware that some particular significance lay behind them. He had the feeling that she was leaving some part of the story untold—and a stronger feeling that, for some reason, she wanted him to be aware of the fact.

There was a silence—a long and rather difficult silence. Luke felt like an actor who does not know his cue. He said rather weakly:

"And you don't think it was suicide?"

Miss Waynflete said promptly:

"Certainly not. If the girl had decided to make away with herself, she would have bought something probably. This was an old bottle of stuff that she must have had for years. And anyway, as I've told you, she wasn't that *kind* of girl."

"So you think—what?" said Luke bluntly.

Miss Waynflete said:

"I think it was very unfortunate."

She closed her lips and looked at him earnestly.

Just when Luke was feeling that he must try desperately to say something anticipated, a diversion occurred. There was a scratching at the door and a plaintive mew.

Miss Waynflete sprang up and went to open the door, whereupon a magnificent orange Persian walked in. He paused, looked disapprovingly at the visitor, and sprang upon the arm of Miss Waynflete's chair.

Miss Waynflete addressed him in a cooing voice.

" Why, Wonky Pooh—where's my Wonky Pooh been all the morning?"

The name struck a chord of memory. Where had he heard something about a Persian cat called Wonky Pooh. He said:

" That's a very handsome cat. Have you had him long?"

Miss Waynflete shook her head.

" Oh, no, he belonged to an old friend of mine, Miss Pinkerton. She was run over by one of these horrid motor-cars and of course I couldn't have let Wonky Pooh go to strangers. Lavinia would have been most upset. She simply worshipped him—and he is very beautiful isn't he?"

Luke admired the cat gravely.

Miss Waynflete said: " Be careful of his ears. They've been rather painful lately."

Luke stroked the animal warily.

Bridget rose to her feet.

She said, " We must be going."

Miss Waynflete shook hands with Luke.

" Perhaps," she said, " I shall see you again before long."

Luke said cheerfully: " I hope so, I'm sure."

He thought she looked puzzled and a little disappointed. Her gaze shifted to Bridget—a rapid look with a hint of interrogation in it. Luke felt that there was some understanding between the two women from which he was excluded. It annoyed him, but he promised himself to get to the bottom of it before long.

Miss Waynflete came out with them. Luke stood a minute on the top of the steps looking with approval on the untouched primness of the village-green and the duck pond.

" Marvellously unspoilt, this place," he said.

Miss Waynflete's face lit up.

" Yes, indeed," she said eagerly. " Really it is still just as

I remember it as a child. We lived in the Hall, you know. But when it came to my brother he did not care to live in it —indeed could not afford to do so, and it was put up for sale. A builder had made an offer and was, I believe, going to ' develop the land,' I think that was the phrase. Fortunately, Lord Whitfield stepped in and acquired the property and saved it. He turned the house into a library and museum—really it is practically untouched. I act as librarian twice a week there —unpaid, *of course*—and I can't tell you what a pleasure it is to be in the old place and know that it will not be vandalised. And really it *is* a perfect setting—you must visit our little museum one day, Mr. Fitzwilliam. There are some quite interesting local exhibits."

"I certainly shall make a point of doing so, Miss Waynflete."

"Lord Whitfield has been a great benefactor to Wychwood," said Miss Waynflete. "It grieves me that there are people who are sadly ungrateful."

Her lips pressed themselves together. Luke discreetly asked no questions. He said good-bye again.

When they were outside the gate Bridget said:

"Do you want to pursue further researches or shall we go home by way of the river. It's a pleasant walk."

Luke answered promptly. He had no mind for further investigations with Bridget Conway standing by listening. He said:

"Go round by the river, by all means."

They walked along the High Street. One of the last houses had a sign decorated in old gold lettering with the word Antiques on it. Luke paused and peered through one of the windows into the cool depths.

"Rather a nice slipware dish there," he remarked. "Do for an aunt of mine. Wonder how much they want for it?"

"Shall we go in and see?"

"Do you mind? I like pottering about antique shops. Sometimes one picks up a good bargain."

"I doubt if you will here," said Bridget dryly. "Ellsworthy knows the value of his stuff pretty accurately, I should say."

The door was open. In the hall were chairs and settees and

dressers with china and pewter on them. Two rooms full of goods opened at either side.

Luke went into the room on the left and picked up the slipware dish. At the same moment a dim figure came forward from the back of the room where he had been sitting at a Queen Anne walnut desk.

"Ah, dear Miss Conway, what a pleasure to see you."

"Good morning, Mr. Ellsworthy."

Mr. Ellsworthy was a very exquisite young man dressed in a colour scheme of russet brown. He had a long pale face with a womanish mouth, long black artistic hair and a mincing walk.

Luke was introduced and Mr. Ellsworthy immediately transferred his attention to him.

"Genuine old English slipware. Delicious, isn't it? I love my bits and pieces, you know, hate to sell them. It's always been my dream to live in the country and a have a little shop. Marvellous place, Wychwood—it has atmosphere, if you know what I mean."

"The artistic temperament," murmured Bridget.

Ellsworthy turned on her with a flash of long white hands.

"Not that terrible phrase, Miss Conway. No—no, I implore you. Don't tell me I'm all arty and crafty—I couldn't bear it. Really, really, you know, I don't stock hand-woven tweeds and beaten pewter. I'm a tradesman, that's all, just a tradesman."

"But you're really an artist, aren't you?" said Luke. "I mean, you do water-colours, don't you?"

"Now who told you that?" cried Mr. Ellsworthy, clasping his hands together. "You know this place is really too marvellous—one simply can't keep a secret! That's what I like about it—it's so different from that inhuman you-mind-your-own-business-and-I will-mind-mine of a city! Gossip and malice and scandal—all so delicious if one takes them in the right spirit!"

Luke contented himself with answering Mr. Ellsworthy's question and paying no attention to the latter part of his remarks.

"Miss Waynflete told us that you had made several sketches of a girl—Amy Gibbs."

"Oh, Amy," said Mr. Ellsworthy. He took a step backwards and set a beer mug rocking. He steadied it carefully. He said: "Did I? Oh, yes, I suppose I did."

His poise seemed somewhat shaken.

"She was a pretty girl," said Bridget.

Mr. Ellsworthy had recovered his aplomb.

"Oh, do you think so?" he asked. "Very commonplace, I always thought. If you're interested in slipware," he went on to Luke, "I've got a couple of slipware birds—delicious things."

Luke displayed a faint interest in the birds and then asked the price of the dish.

Ellsworthy named a figure.

"Thanks," said Luke, "but I don't think I'll deprive you of it after all."

"I'm always relieved, you know," said Ellsworthy, "when I don't make a sale. Foolish of me, isn't it? Look here, I'll let you have it for a guinea less. You care for the stuff. I can see that —it makes all the difference. And after all, this *is* a shop!"

"No, thanks," said Luke.

Mr. Ellsworthy accompanied them out to the door, waving his hands—very unpleasant hands, Luke thought they were— the flesh seemed not so much white as faintly greenish.

"Nasty bit of goods, Mr. Ellsworthy," he remarked when he and Bridget were out of earshot.

"A nasty mind and nasty habits I should say," said Bridget.

"Why does he really come to a place like this?"

"I believe he dabbles in black magic. Not quite black Masses but that sort of thing. The reputation of this place helps."

Luke said rather awkwardly: "Good lord—I suppose he's the kind of chap I really need. I ought to have talked to him on the subject."

"Do you think so?" said Bridget. "He knows a lot about it."

Luke said rather uneasily:

"I'll look him up some other day."

Bridget did not answer. They were out of the town now. She turned aside to follow a footpath and presently they came to the river.

There they passed a small man with a stiff moustache and protuberant eyes. He had three bulldogs with him to whom he was shouting hoarsely in turn. "Nero, come here, sir. Nelly, leave it. Drop it, I tell you. Augustus—AUGUSTUS, I say——"

He broke off to raise his hat to Bridget, stared at Luke with what was evidently a devouring curiosity and passed on resuming his hoarse expostulations.

"Major Horton and his bulldogs?" quoted Luke.

"Quite right."

"Haven't we seen practically every one of note in Wychwood this morning?"

"Practically."

"I feel rather obtrusive," said Luke. "I suppose a stranger in an English village is bound to stick out a mile," he added ruefully remembering Jimmy Lorrimer's remarks.

"Major Horton never disguises his curiosity very well," said Bridget. "He did stare, rather."

"He's the sort of man you could tell was a Major anywhere," said Luke rather viciously.

Bridget said abruptly: "Shall we sit on the bank a bit? We've got lots of time."

They sat on a fallen tree that made a convenient seat. Bridget went on:

"Yes, Major Horton is very military—has an orderly room manner. You'd hardly believe he was the most hen-pecked man in existence a year ago!"

"What, that fellow?"

"Yes. He had the most disagreeable woman for a wife that I've ever known. She had the money too, and never scrupled to underline the fact in public."

"Poor brute—Horton, I mean."

"He behaved very nicely to her—always the officer and gentleman. Personally, I wonder he didn't take a hatchet to her."

"She wasn't popular, I gather."

"Everybody disliked her. She snubbed Gordon and patronised me and made herself generally unpleasant wherever she went."

"But I gather a merciful providence removed her?"

"Yes, about a year ago. Acute gastritis. She gave her husband, Dr. Thomas and two nurses absolute Hell—but she died all right! The bulldogs brightened up at once."

"Intelligent brutes!"

There was a silence. Bridget was idly picking at the long grass. Luke frowned at the opposite bank unseeingly. Once again the dreamlike quality of his mission obsessed him. How much was fact—how much imagination? Wasn't it bad for one to go about studying every fresh person you met as a potential murderer? Something degrading about that point of view.

"Damn it all," thought Luke, "I've been a policeman too long!"

He was brought out of his abstraction with a shock. Bridget's cold clear voice was speaking.

"Mr. Fitzwilliam," she said, "just exactly why have you come down here?"

CHAPTER SIX

Hat Paint

LUKE HAD been just in the act of applying a match to a cigarette. The unexpectedness of her remark momentarily paralysed his hand. He remained quite motionless for a second or two, the match burned down and scorched his fingers.

"Damn," said Luke as he dropped the match and shook his hand vigorously. "I beg your pardon. You gave me rather a nasty jolt." He smiled ruefully.

"Did I?"

"Yes." He sighed. "Oh, well, I suppose any one of real intelligence was bound to see through me! That story of my writing a book on folklore didn't take you in for a moment, I suppose?"

"Not after I'd once seen you."

"You believed it up to then?"

"Yes."

"All the same it wasn't really a good story," said Luke critically. "I mean, any man might want to write a book, but the bit about coming down here and passing myself off as a cousin—I suppose that made you smell a rat?"

Bridget shook her head.

"No. I had an explanation for that—I thought I had, I mean. I presumed you were pretty hard up—a lot of my and Jimmy's friends are that—and I thought he suggested the cousin stunt so that—well so that it would save your pride."

"But when I arrived," said Luke. "My appearance immediately suggested such opulence that that explanation was out of the question?"

Her mouth curved in its slow smile.

"Oh, no," she said. "It wasn't that. It was simply that you were the wrong kind of person."

"Not sufficient brains to write a book? Don't spare my feelings. I'd rather know."

"You might write a book—but not that *kind* of book—old superstitions—delving into the past—not that sort of thing! You're not the kind of man to whom the past means much—perhaps not even the future—only just the present."

"H'm—I see." He made a wry face. "Damn it all, you've made me nervous ever since I got here! You look so confoundedly intelligent."

"I'm sorry," said Bridget dryly. "What did you expect?"

"Well, I really hadn't thought about it."

But she went on calmly:

"A fluffy little person—with just enough brains to realise her opportunities and marry her boss?"

Luke made a confused noise. She turned a cool amused glance on him.

"I quite understand. It's all right. I'm not annoyed."

Luke chose effrontery.

"Well, perhaps, it was something faintly approaching that. But I didn't think much about it."

She said slowly:

"No, you wouldn't. You don't cross your fences till you get to them."

But Luke was despondent.

"Oh, I've no doubt I did my stuff pretty rottenly! Has Lord Whitfield seen through me too?"

"Oh, no. If you said you'd come down here to study the habits of water beetles and write a monograph about them, it would have been O.K. with Gordon. He's got a beautiful believing mind."

"All the same I wasn't a bit convincing! I got rattled somehow."

"I cramped your style," said Bridget. "I saw that. It rather amused me, I'm afraid."

"Oh, it would! Women with any brains are usually cold-bloodedly cruel."

Bridget murmured:

"One has to take one's pleasures as one can in this life!" She paused a minute, then said: "Why are you down here, Mr. Fitzwilliam?"

They had returned full circle to the original question. Luke had been aware that it must be so. In the last few seconds he had been trying to make up his mind. He looked up now and met her eyes—shrewd inquiring eyes that met his with a calm, steady gaze. There was a gravity in them which he had not quite expected to find there.

"It would be better, I think," he said meditatively, "not to tell you any more lies."

"Much better."

"But the truth's awkward. . . . Look here, have you your-self formed any opinion—I mean has anything occurred to you about my being here?"

She nodded slowly and thoughtfully.

"What was your idea? Will you tell me? I fancy it may help somehow."

Bridget said quietly:

"I had an idea that you came down here in connection with the death of that girl, Amy Gibbs."

"That's it, then! That's what I saw—what I felt—when-ever her name cropped up! I *knew* there was something. So you thought I came down about that?"

"Didn't you?"

"In a way—yes."

He was silent—frowning. The girl beside him sat equally

silent, not moving. She said nothing to disturb his train of thought.

He made up his mind.

" I've come down here on a wild goose chase—on a fantastical and probably quite absurd and melodramatic supposition. Amy Gibbs is part of that whole business. I'm interested to find out exactly how she died."

" Yes, I thought so."

" But dash it all—*why* did you think so? What is there about her death that—well—aroused your interest?"

Bridget said:

" I've thought—all along—that there was something wrong about it. That's why I took you to see Miss Waynflete."

" Why?"

" Because she thinks so too."

" Oh." Luke thought back rapidly. He understood now the underlying suggestions of that intelligent spinster's manner. " She thinks as you do—that there's something—odd about it?"

Bridget nodded.

" Why exactly?"

" Hat paint, to begin with."

" What do you mean, hat paint?"

" Well, about twenty years ago, people *did* paint hats—one season you had a pink straw, next season a bottle of hat paint and it became dark blue—then perhaps another bottle and a black hat! But nowadays—hats are cheap—tawdry stuff to be thrown away when out of fashion."

" Even girls of the class of Amy Gibbs?"

" I'd be more likely to paint a hat than she would! Thrift's gone out. And there's another thing. It was *red* hat paint."

" Well?"

" And Amy Gibbs had red hair—carrots!"

" You mean it doesn't go together?"

Bridget nodded.

" You wouldn't wear a scarlet hat with carroty hair. It's the sort of thing a man wouldn't realise, but——"

Luke interrupted her with heavy significance.

" No—a *man* wouldn't realise that. It fits in—it all fits in."

Bridget said:

" Jimmy has got some odd friends at Scotland Yard. You're not——"

Luke said quickly:

" I'm not an official detective—and I'm not a well-known private investigator with rooms in Baker Street, etc. I'm exactly what Jimmy told you I was—a retired policeman from the East. I'm horning in on this business because of an odd thing that happened in the train to London."

He gave a brief synopsis of his conversation with Miss Pinkerton and the subsequent events which had brought about his presence in Wychwood.

" So you see," he ended. " It's fantastic! I'm looking for a certain man—a secret killer—a man here in Wychwood—probably well-known and respected. If Miss Pinkerton's right and you're right and Miss What's-'er-name is right—that man killed Amy Gibbs."

Bridget said: " I see."

" It could have been done from outside, I suppose?"

" Yes, I think so," said Bridget slowly. " Reed, the constable climbed up to her window by means of an outhouse. The window was open. It was a bit of a scramble, but a reasonably active man would find no real difficulty."

" And having done that, he did what?"

" Substituted a bottle of hat paint for the cough linctus."

" Hoping she'd do exactly what she did do—wake up, drink it off, and that every one would say she'd made a mistake or committed suicide?"

" Yes."

" There was no suspicion of what they call in books, ' foul play' at the inquest?"

" No."

" Men again, I suppose—the hat paint point wasn't raised?"

" No."

" But it occurred to you?"

" Yes."

" And to Miss Waynflete? Have you discussed it together?"
Bridget smiled faintly.

" Oh, no—not in the sense you mean. I mean we haven't

said anything right out. I don't really know how far the old pussy has gone in her own mind. I'd say she'd been just worried to start with—and gradually getting more so. She's quite intelligent, you know, went to Girton or wanted to, and was advanced when she was young. She's not got quite the woolly mind of most of the people down here."

"Miss Pinkerton had rather a woolly mind I should imagine," said Luke. "That's why I never dreamed there was anything in her story to begin with."

"She was pretty shrewd, I always thought," said Bridget. "Most of these rambling old dears are as sharp as nails in some ways. You said she mentioned other names?"

Luke nodded.

"Yes. A small boy—that was Tommy Pierce—I remembered the name as soon as I heard it. And I'm pretty sure that the man Carter came in too."

"Carter, Tommy Pierce, Amy Gibbs, Dr. Humbleby," said Bridget thoughtfully. "As you say, it's almost too fantastic to be true! Who on earth would want to kill those people. They were all so different!"

Luke asked:

"Any idea as to why any one should want to do away with Amy Gibbs?"

Bridget shook her head.

"I can't imagine."

"What about the man Carter? How did he die, by the way?"

"Fell into the river and was drowned. He was on his way home, it was a misty night and he was quite drunk. There's a footbridge with a rail on only one side. It was taken for granted that he missed his footing."

"But some one *could* quite easily have given him a shove?"

"Oh, yes."

"And somebody else could quite easily have given nasty little Tommy a push when he was window cleaning?"

"Again yes."

"So it boils down to the fact that it's really quite easy to remove three human beings without any one suspecting."

"Miss Pinkerton suspected," Bridget pointed out.

"So she did, bless her. *She* wasn't troubled with ideas of being too melodramatic, or of imagining things."

"She often told me the world was a very wicked place."

"And you smiled tolerantly, I suppose?"

"In a superior manner!"

"Anybody who can believe six impossible things before breakfast wins hands down at this game."

Bridget nodded.

Luke said:

"I suppose it's no good my asking you if you've a hunch of any kind? There's no particular individual in Wychwood who gives you a creepy feeling down the spine, or who has strange pale eyes—or a queer maniacal giggle."

"Everybody I've met in Wychwood appears to me to be eminently sane, respectable, and completely ordinary."

"I was afraid you'd say that," said Luke.

Bridget said:

"You think this man is definitely mad?"

"Oh, I should say so. A lunatic all right, but a cunning one. The last person you'd ever suggest—probably a pillar of society like the Bank Manager."

"Mr. Jones? I certainly can't imagine him committing wholesale murders."

"Then he's probably the man we want."

"It may be any one," said Bridget. "The butcher, the baker, the grocer, a farm labourer, a road-mender, or the man who delivers the milk."

"It may be—yes—but I think the field is a little more restricted than that."

"Why?"

"My Miss Pinkerton spoke of the look in his eyes when he was measuring up his next victim. From the way she spoke I got the impression—it's only an impression, mark you— that the man she was speaking of was at least her social equal. Of course, I may be wrong."

"You're probably quite right! Those *nuances* of conversation can't be put down in black and white, but they're the sort of things one doesn't really make mistakes about."

"You know," said Luke, "it's a great relief to have you knowing all about it."

" It will probably cramp your style less, I agree. And I can probably help you."

" Your help will be invaluable. You really mean to see it through?"

" Of course."

Luke said with a sudden slight embarrassment:

" What about Lord Whitfield? Do you think——?"

" Naturally we don't tell Gordon anything about it!" said Bridget.

" You mean he wouldn't believe it?"

" Oh, he'd *believe* it! Gordon could believe anything! He'd probably be simply thrilled and insist on having half a dozen of his bright young men down to beat up the neighbourhood! He'd simply adore it!"

" That does rather rule it out," agreed Luke.

" Yes, we can't allow him to have his simple pleasures, I'm afraid."

Luke looked at her. He seemed about to say something then changed his mind. He looked instead at his watch.

" Yes," said Bridget, " we ought to be getting home."

She got up. There was a sudden constraint between them as though Luke's unspoken words hovered uncomfortably in the air.

They walked home in silence.

CHAPTER SEVEN

Possibilities

LUKE SAT in his bedroom. At lunch time he had sustained an interrogation by Mrs. Anstruther as to what flowers he had had in his garden in the Mayang Straits. He had then been told what flowers would have done well there. He had also listened to further " Talks to Young Men on the Subject of Myself " by Lord Whitfield. Now he was mercifully alone.

He took a sheet of paper and wrote down a series of names. It ran as follows:

Dr. Thomas.
Mr. Abbot.
Major Horton.
Mr. Ellsworthy.
Mr. Wake.
Mr. Jones.
Amy's young man.
The butcher, the baker, the candlestick maker, etc.

He then took another sheet of paper and headed it VICTIMS. Under this heading, he wrote:

Amy Gibbs: Poisoned.
Tommy Pierce: Pushed out of window.
Harry Carter: Shoved off footbridge (drunk?
                       drugged?).
Dr. Humbleby: Blood poisoning.
Miss Pinkerton: Run down by car.

He added:

Mrs. Rose?
Old Ben?

And after a pause:

Mrs. Horton?

He considered his lists, smoked awhile, then took up his pencil once more.

Dr. Thomas: Possible case against him.
    Definite motive in the case of Dr. Humbleby. Manner
    of latter's death suitable—namely, scientific poisoning
    by germs. Amy Gibbs visited him on afternoon of
    the day she died. (Anything between them? Black-
    mail?)
    Tommy Pierce? No connection known. (Did Tommy
    know of connection between him and Amy Gibbs?)
    Harry Carter? No connection known.

Was Dr. Thomas absent from Wychwood on the day Miss Pinkerton went to London?

Luke sighed and started a fresh heading:

Mr. Abbot: Possible case against him.
(Feel a lawyer is definitely a suspicious person. Possibly prejudice.) His personality, florid, genial, etc., would be definitely suspicious in a book—always suspect bluff genial men. Objection: this is not a book, but real life.
Motive for murder of Dr. Humbleby. Definite antagonism existed between them. H. defied Abbot. Sufficient motive for a deranged brain. Antagonism could have been easily noted by Miss Pinkerton.
Tommy Pierce? Latter snooped among Abbot's papers. Did he find out something he shouldn't have known?
Harry Carter? No definite connection.
Amy Gibbs? No connection known. Hat paint quite suitable to Abbot's mentality—an old-fashioned mind. Was Abbot away from the village the day Miss Pinkerton was killed?

Major Horton: Possible case against him.
No connection known with Amy Gibbs, Tommy Pierce or Carter.
What about Mrs. Horton? Death sounds as though it might be arsenical poisoning. If so other murders might be result of that—blackmail? N.B.—Thomas was doctor in attendance. (Suspicious for Thomas again.)

Mr. Ellsworthy: Possible case against him.
Nasty bit of goods—dabbles in black magic. Might be temperament of a blood lust killer. Connection with Amy Gibbs. Any connection with Tommy Pierce? Carter? Nothing known. Humbleby? Might have tumbled to Ellsworthy's mental condition. Miss Pinkerton? Was Ellsworthy away from Wychwood when Miss Pinkerton was killed?

Mr. Wake: Possible case against him.
> Very unlikely. Possible religious mania? A mission to kill? Saintly old clergymen likely starters in books, but (as before) this is real life.
> Note. Carter, Tommy, Amy all definitely unpleasant characters. Better removed by divine decree?

Mr. Jones.
> Data—none.

Amy's young man.
> Probably every reason to kill Amy—but seems unlikely on general grounds.

The etceteras?
> Don't fancy them.

He read through what he had written.
Then he shook his head.
He murmured softly :
" —which is absurd ! How nicely Euclid put things."
He tore up the lists and burnt them.
He said to himself :
" This job isn't going to be exactly easy."

CHAPTER EIGHT

Dr. Thomas

DR. THOMAS leant back in his chair, and passed a long delicate hand over his thick fair hair. He was a young man whose appearance was deceptive. Though he was over thirty, a casual glance would have put him down in the early twenties if not in his teens. His shock of rather unruly fair hair, his slightly startled expression and his pink and white complexion gave him an irresistibly school-boyish appearance. Immature as he might look, though, the diagnosis he had just pronounced on Luke's rheumatic knee agreed almost precisely with that delivered by an eminent Harley Street specialist only a week earlier.

" Thanks," said Luke. " Well, I'm relieved you think that electrical treatment will do the trick. I don't want to turn a cripple at my age."

Dr. Thomas smiled boyishly.

" Oh, I don't think there's any danger of that, Mr. Fitzwilliam."

" Well, you've relieved my mind," said Luke. " I was thinking of going to some specialist chap—but I'm sure there's no need now."

Dr. Thomas smiled again.

" Go if it makes your mind easier. After all, it's always a good thing to have an expert's opinion."

" No, no, I've got full confidence in you."

" Frankly, there is no complexity about the matter. If you take my advice, I am quite sure you will have no further trouble."

" You've relieved my mind no end, doctor. Fancied I might be getting arthritis and would soon be all tied up in knots and unable to move."

Dr. Thomas shook his head with a slightly indulgent smile.

Luke said quickly :

" Men get the wind up pretty badly in these ways. I expect you find that? I often think a doctor must feel himself a ' medicine man '—a kind of magician to most of his patients."

" The element of faith enters in very largely."

" I know. ' The doctor says so ' is a remark always uttered with something like reverence."

Dr. Thomas raised his shoulders.

" If one's patients only knew ! " he murmured humorously. Then he said :

" You're writing a book on magic, aren't you, Mr. Fitzwilliam?"

" Now how did you know that?" exclaimed Luke, perhaps with somewhat overdone surprise.

Dr. Thomas looked amused.

" Oh, my dear sir, news gets about very rapidly in a place like this. We have so little to talk about."

" It probably gets exaggerated too. You'll be hearing I'm raising the local spirits and emulating the Witch of Endor."

" Rather odd you should say that."

" Why?"

" Well, the rumour has been going round that you had raised the ghost of Tommy Pierce."

" Pierce? Pierce? Is that the small boy who fell out of a window?"

" Yes."

" Now I wonder how—of course—I made some remark to the solicitor—what's his name, Abbot."

" Yes, the story originated with Abbot."

" Don't say I've converted a hard-boiled solicitor to a belief in ghosts?"

" You believe in ghosts yourself, then?"

" Your tone suggests that you do not, doctor. No, I wouldn't say I actually ' believe in ghosts '—to put it crudely. But I have known curious phenomena in the case of sudden or violent death. But I'm more interested in the various superstitions pertaining to violent deaths—that a murdered man, for instance, can't rest in his grave. And the interesting belief that the blood of a murdered man flows if his murderer touches him. I wonder how that arose."

" Very curious," said Thomas. " But I don't suppose many people remember that nowadays."

" More than you would think. Of course, I don't suppose you have many murders down here—so it's hard to judge."

Luke had smiled as he spoke, his eyes resting with seeming carelessness on the other's face. But Dr. Thomas seemed quite unperturbed and smiled in return.

" No, I don't think we've had a murder for—oh, very many years—certainly not in my time."

" No, this is a peaceful spot. Not conducive to foul play. Unless somebody pushed little Tommy What's-his-name out of the window."

Luke laughed. Again Dr. Thomas's smile came in answer —a natural smile full of boyish amusement.

" A lot of people would have been willing to wring that child's neck," he said. " But I don't think they actually got to the point of throwing him out of windows."

" He seems to have been a thoroughly nasty child—the removal of him might have been conceived as a public duty."

" It's a pity one can't apply that theory fairly often."

"I've always thought a few wholesale murders would be beneficial to the community," said Luke. "A club bore, for instance, should be finished off with a poisoned liqueur brandy. Then there are the women who gush at you and tear all their dearest friends to pieces with their tongues. Back-biting spinsters. Inveterate diehards who oppose progress. If they were painlessly removed, what a difference it would make to social life!"

Dr. Thomas's smile lengthened to a grin.

"In fact, you advocate crime on a grand scale?"

"Judicious elimination," said Luke. "Don't you agree that it would be beneficial?"

"Oh, undoubtedly."

"Ah, but you're not being serious," said Luke. "Now I am. I haven't the respect for human life that the normal Englishman has. Any man who is a stumbling block on the way of progress ought to be eliminated—that's how I see it!"

Running his hand through his short fair hair, Dr. Thomas said:

"Yes, but who is to be the judge of a man's fitness or unfitness?"

"That's the difficulty, of course," Luke admitted.

"The Catholics would consider a Communist agitator unfit to live—the Communist agitator would sentence the priest to death as a purveyor of superstition, the doctor would eliminate the unhealthy man, the pacifist would condemn the soldier, and so on."

"You'd have to have a scientific man as judge," said Luke. "Some one with an unbiased but highly specialised mind—a doctor, for instance. Come to that, I think you'd be a pretty good judge yourself, doctor."

"Of unfitness to live?"

"Yes."

Dr. Thomas shook his head.

"My job is to make the unfit fit. Most of the time it's an uphill job, I'll admit."

"Now just for the sake of argument," said Luke. "Take a man like the late Harry Carter——"

Dr. Thomas said sharply:

"Carter? You mean the landlord of the Seven Stars?"

"Yes, that's the man. I never knew him myself, but my cousin, Miss Conway, was talking about him. He seems to have been a really thorough-going scoundrel."

"Well," said the other, "he drank, of course. Ill-treated his wife, bullied his daughter. He was quarrelsome and abusive and had had a row with most people in the place."

"In fact, the world is a better place without him?"

"One might be inclined to say so, I agree."

"In fact, if somebody had given him a push and sent him into the river instead of his kindly electing to fall in of his own accord, that person would have been acting in the public interest?"

Dr. Thomas said dryly:

"These methods that you advocate—did you put them into practice in the—Mayang Straits, I think you said?"

Luke laughed.

"Oh, no, with me it's theory—not practice."

"No, I do not think you are the stuff of which murderers are made."

Luke asked:

"Why not? I've been frank enough in my views."

"Exactly. Too frank."

"You mean that if I were really the kind of man who takes the law into his own hands I shouldn't go about airing my views?"

"That was my meaning."

"But it might be a kind of gospel with me. I might be a fanatic on the subject!"

"Even so, your sense of self-protection would be active."

"In fact, when looking for a murderer, look out for a nice gentle wouldn't-hurt-a-fly type of man."

"Slightly exaggerated perhaps," said Dr. Thomas, "but not far from the truth."

Luke said abruptly:

"Tell me—it interests me—have you ever come across a man whom you believed might be a murderer?"

Dr. Thomas said sharply:

"Really—what an extraordinary question!"

"Is it? After all, a doctor must come across so many queer

characters. He would be better able to detect—for instance—
the signs of homicidal mania—in an early stage—before it's
noticeable."

Thomas said rather irritably:

" You have the general layman's idea of a homicidal maniac
—a man who runs amok with a knife, a man more or less
foaming at the mouth. Let me tell you a homicidal lunatic may
be the most difficult thing on this earth to spot. To all seeming
he may be exactly like every one else—a man, perhaps, who is
easily frightened—who may tell you, perhaps, that he has
enemies. No more than that. A quiet, inoffensive fellow."

" Is that really so?"

" Of course it's so. A homicidal lunatic often kills (as he
thinks) in self-defence. But of course a lot of killers are
ordinary sane fellows like you and me."

" Doctor, you alarm me! Fancy if you should discover later
that I have five or six nice quiet little killings to my credit."

Dr. Thomas smiled.

" I don't think it's very likely, Mr. Fitzwilliam."

" Don't you? I'll return the compliment. I don't believe
you've got five or six murders to your credit either."

Dr. Thomas said cheerfully:

" You're not counting my professional failures."

Both men laughed.

Luke got up and said good-bye.

" I'm afraid I've taken up a lot of your time," he said apologetically.

" Oh, I'm not busy. Wychwood is a pretty healthy place.
It's a pleasure to have a talk with some one from the outside
world."

" I was wondering——" said Luke and stopped.

" Yes?"

" Miss Conway told me when she sent me to you what a
very—well—what a first-class man you were. I wondered if
you didn't feel rather buried down here? Not much opportunity for talent."

" Oh, general practice is a good beginning. It's valuable
experience."

" But you won't be content to stay in a rut all your life?

Your late partner, Dr. Humbleby, was an unambitious fellow,
so I've heard—quite content with his practice here. He'd
been here for a good many years, I believe?"

" Practically a lifetime."

" He was sound but old-fashioned, so I hear."

Dr. Thomas said:

" At times he was difficult. . . . Very suspicious of modern
innovations, but a good example of the old school of physic-
ians."

" Left a very pretty daughter, I'm told," said Luke in jocular
fashion.

He had the pleasure of seeing Dr. Thomas's pale-pink
countenance go a deep scarlet.

" Oh—er—yes," he said.

Luke gazed at him kindly. He was pleased at the prospect
of erasing Dr. Thomas from his list of suspected persons.

The latter recovered his normal hue and said abruptly:

" Talking about crime just now, I can lend you rather a
good book as you are interested in the subject! Translation
from the German. Kreuzhammer on *Inferiority and Crime.*"

" Thank you," said Luke.

Dr. Thomas ran his finger along a shelf and drew out the
book in question.

" Here you are. Some of the theories are rather startling—
and of course they are only theories, but they are interesting.
The early life of Menzheld, for instance, the Frankfurt butcher,
as they called him, and the chapter on Anna Helm, the little
nursemaid killer, are really extremely interesting."

" She killed about a dozen of her charges before the authorities tumbled to it, I believe," said Luke.

Dr. Thomas nodded.

" Yes. She had a most sympathetic personality—devoted
to children—and apparently quite genuinely heartbroken at
each death. The psychology is amazing."

" Amazing how these people get away with it," said Luke.

He was on the doorstep now. Dr. Thomas had come out
with him.

" Not amazing really," said Dr. Thomas. " It's quite easy,
you know."

" What is?"

" To get away with it." He was smiling again—a charming, boyish smile. " If you're careful. One just has to be careful—that's all! But a clever man *is* extremely careful not to make a slip. That's all there is to it."

He smiled and went into the house.

Luke stood staring up the steps.

There had been something condescending in the doctor's smile. Throughout their conversation Luke had been conscious of himself as a man of full maturity and of Dr. Thomas as a youthful and ingenuous young man.

Just for a moment he felt the rôles reversed. The doctor's smile had been that of a grown-up amused by the cleverness of a child.

CHAPTER NINE

Mrs. Pierce Talks

IN THE little shop in the High Street Luke had bought a tin of cigarettes and to-day's copy of *Good Cheer,* the enterprising little weekly which provided Lord Whitfield with a good portion of his substantial income. Turning to the football competition, Luke, with a groan, gave forth the information that he had just failed to win a hundred and twenty pounds. Mrs. Pierce was roused at once to sympathy and explained similar disappointments on the part of her husband. Friendly relations thus established, Luke found no difficulty in prolonging the conversation.

" A great interest in football Mr. Pierce takes," said Mr. Pierce's spouse. " Turns to it first of all in the news, he does. And as I say, many a disappointment he's had, but there, everybody can't win, that's what I say, and what I say is you can't go against luck."

Luke concurred heartily in these sentiments, and proceeded to advance by an easy transition to a further profound statement that troubles never come singly.

" Ah, no, indeed, sir, that I *do* know." Mrs. Pierce sighed. " And when a woman has a husband and eight children—six living and buried two, that is—well, she knows what trouble is, as you may say."

"I suppose she does—oh, undoubtedly," said Luke. "You've —er—buried two, you say?"

"One no longer than a month ago," said Mrs. Pierce with a kind of melancholy enjoyment.

"Dear me, very sad."

"It wasn't only sad, sir. It was a shock—that's what it was, a shock! I came all over queer, I did, when they broke it to me. Never having expected anything of that kind to happen to Tommy, as you might say, for when a boy's a trouble to you it doesn't come natural to think of him being took. Now my Emma Jane, a sweet little mite she was. 'You'll never rear her.' That's what they said. 'She's too good to live.' And it was true, sir. The Lord knows His own."

Luke acknowledged the sentiment and strove to return from the subject of the saintly Emma Jane to that of the less saintly Tommy.

"Your boy died quite recently?" he said. "An accident?"

"An accident it was, sir. Cleaning the windows of the old Hall, which is now the library, and he must have lost his balance and fell—from the top windows, that was."

Mrs. Pierce expatiated at some length on all the details of the accident.

"Wasn't there some story," said Luke carelessly, "of his having been seen dancing on the window-sill?"

Mrs. Pierce said that boys would be boys—but no doubt it did give the major a turn, him being a fussy gentleman.

"Major Horton?"

"Yes, sir, the gentleman with the bulldogs. After the accident happened he chanced to mention having seen our Tommy acting very rash-like—and of course it does show that if something sudden had startled him he would have fallen easy enough. High spirits, sir, that was Tommy's trouble. A sore trial he's been to me in many ways," she finished, "but there it was, just high spirits—nothing but high spirits —such as any lad might have. There wasn't no real harm in him, as you might say."

"No, no—I'm sure there wasn't, but sometimes, you know,

Mrs. Pierce, people—sober middle-aged people—find it hard to remember they've ever been young themselves."

Mrs. Pierce sighed.

"Very true those words are, sir. I can't help but hoping that some gentlemen I could name but won't will have taken it to heart the way they were hard upon the lad—just on account of his high spirits."

"Played a few tricks upon his employers, did he?" asked Luke with an indulgent smile.

Mrs. Pierce responded immediately.

"It was just his fun, sir, that was all. Tommy was always good at imitations. Make us hold our sides with laughing the way he'd mince about pretending to be that Mr. Ellsworthy at the curio shop—or old Mr. Hobbs, the churchwarden—and he was imitating his lordship up at the manor and the two under-gardeners laughing, when up came his lordship quiet-like and gave Tommy the sack on the spot—and naturally that was only to be expected, and quite right, and his lordship didn't bear malice afterwards, and helped Tommy to get another job."

"But other people weren't so magnanimous, eh?" said Luke.

"That they were not, sir. Naming no names. And you'd never think it with Mr. Abbot, so pleasant in his manner and always a kind word or a joke."

"Tommy got into trouble with him?"

Mrs. Pierce said:

"It's not, I'm sure, that the boy meant any harm. . . . And after all, if papers are private and not meant to be looked at, they shouldn't be laid out on a table—that's what I say."

"Oh, quite," said Luke. "Private papers in a lawyer's office ought to be kept in the safe."

"That's right, sir. That's what I think, and Mr. Pierce he agrees with me. It's not even as though Tommy had read much of it."

"What was it—a will?" asked Luke.

He judged (probably rightly) that a question as to what the document in question had been might make Mrs. Pierce halt. But this direct question brought an instant response.

"Oh, no, sir, nothing of that kind. Nothing really important. Just a private letter it was—from a lady—and Tommy didn't even see who the lady was. All such a fuss about nothing —that's what I say."

"Mr. Abbot must be the sort of man who takes offence very easily," said Luke.

"Well, it does seem so, doesn't it, sir? Although, as I say, he's always such a pleasant gentleman to speak to—always a joke or a cheery word. But it's true that I have heard he was a difficult man to get up against, and him and Dr. Humbleby was daggers drawn, as the saying is, just before the poor gentleman died. And not a pleasant thought for Mr. Abbot afterwards. For once there's a death one doesn't like to think there's been harsh words spoken and no chance of taking them back."

Luke shook his head solemnly and murmured:

"Very true—very true."

He went on:

"A bit of a coincidence—that. Hard words with Dr. Humbleby and Dr. Humbleby died—harsh treatment of your Tommy—and the boy dies! I should think that a double experience like that would tend to make Mr. Abbot careful of his tongue in future."

"Harry Carter, too, down at the Seven Stars," said Mrs. Pierce. "Very sharp words passed between them only a week before Carter went and drowned himself—but one can't blame Mr. Abbot for that. The abuse was all on Carter's side—went up to Mr. Abbot's house, he did, being in liquor at the time, and shouting out the foulest language at the top of his voice. Poor Mrs. Carter, she had a deal to put up with, and it must be owned Carter's death was a merciful release as far as she was concerned."

"He left a daughter, too, didn't he?"

"Ah," said Mrs. Pierce. "I'm never one to gossip."

This was unexpected but promising. Luke pricked up his ears and waited.

"I don't say there was anything in it but talk. Lucy Carter's a fine-looking young woman in her way, and if it hadn't been for the difference in station I dare say no notice would have been taken. But talk there has been and you can't deny it—

especially after Carter went right up to his house, shouting and swearing."

Luke gathered the implications of this somewhat confused speech.

" Mr. Abbot looks as though he'd appreciate a good-looking girl," he said.

" It's often the way with gentlemen," said Mrs. Pierce. " They don't mean anything by it—just a word or two in passing, but the gentry's the gentry and it gets noticed in consequence. It's only to be expected in a quiet place like this."

" It's a very charming place," said Luke. " So unspoilt."

" That's what artists always say, but I think we're a bit behind the times myself. Why, there's been no building here to speak of. Over at Ashevale, for instance, they've got a lovely lot of new houses, some of them with green roofs and stained-glass in the windows."

Luke shuddered slightly.

" You've got a grand new institute here," he said.

" They say it's a very fine building," said Mrs. Pierce, without great enthusiasm. " Of course, his lordship's done a lot for the place. He means well, we all know that."

" But you don't think his efforts are quite successful?" said Luke amused.

" Well, of course, sir, he isn't really gentry—not like Miss Waynflete, for instance, and Miss Conway. Why, Lord Whitfield's father kept a boot-shop only a few doors from here. My mother remembers Gordon Ragg serving in the shop—remembers it as well as anything. Of course he's his lordship now and he's a rich man—but it's never the same, is it, sir?"

" Evidently not," said Luke.

" You'll excuse me mentioning it, sir," said Mrs. Pierce. " And of course I know you're staying at the manor and writing a book. But you're a cousin of Miss Bridget's, I know, and that's quite a different thing. Very pleased we shall be to have her back as mistress of Ashe Manor."

" Rather," said Luke. " I'm sure you will."

He paid for his cigarettes and paper with sudden abruptness.

He thought to himself :

" The personal element. One *must* keep that out of it! Hell, I'm here to track down a criminal. What does it matter who that black-haired witch marries or doesn't marry? She doesn't come into this . . ."

He walked slowly along the street. With an effort he thrust Bridget into the back of his mind.

" Now then," he said to himself. " Abbot. The case against Abbot. I've linked him up with three of the victims. He had a row with Humbleby, a row with Carter and a row with Tommy Pierce—and all three died. What about the girl Amy Gibbs? What was the private letter that infernal boy saw? Did he know who it was from? Or didn't he? He mayn't have said so to his mother. But suppose he *did*. Suppose Abbot thought it necessary to shut his mouth. It could be! That's all one can say about it. It could be! Not good enough!"

Luke quickened his pace, looking about him with sudden exasperation.

" This damned village—it's getting on my nerves. So smiling and peaceful—so innocent—and all the time this crazy streak of murder running through it. Or am I the crazy one? Was Lavinia Pinkerton crazy? After all, the whole thing *could* be coincidence—yes, Humbleby's death and all. . . ."

He glanced back down the length of the High Street—and he was assailed by a strong feeling of unreality.

He said to himself:

" These things don't happen. . . ."

Then he lifted his eyes to the long frowning line of Ashe Ridge—and at once the unreality passed. Ashe Ridge was real —it knew strange things—witchcraft and cruelty and forgotten blood lusts and evil rites . . .

He started. Two figures were walking along the side of the ridge. He recognised them easily—Bridget and Ellsworthy. The young man was gesticulating with those curious, unpleasant hands of his. His head was bent to Bridget's. They looked like two figures out of a dream. One felt that their feet made no sound as they sprang cat-like from turf to turf. He saw her black hair stream out behind her blown by the wind. Again that queer magic of hers held him.

" Bewitched, that's what I am, bewitched," he said to himself.

He stood quite still—a queer numbed feeling spreading over him.

He thought to himself ruefully:

"Who's to break the spell? There's no one."

CHAPTER TEN

Rose Humbleby

A SOFT sound behind him made him turn sharply. A girl was standing there, a remarkably pretty girl with brown hair curling round her ears and rather timid-looking dark-blue eyes. She flushed a little with embarrassment before she spoke.

"Mr. Fitzwilliam, isn't it?" she said.

"Yes. I——"

"I'm Rose Humbleby. Bridget told me that—that you knew some people who knew my father."

Luke had the grace to flush slightly under his tan.

"It was a long time ago," he said rather lamely. "They—er—knew him as a young man—before he married."

"Oh, I see."

Rose Humbleby looked a little crestfallen. But she went on:

"You're writing a book, aren't you?"

"Yes. I'm making notes for one, that is. About local superstitions. All that sort of thing."

"I see. It sounds frightfully interesting."

"It will probably be as dull as ditch-water," Luke assured her.

"Oh, no, I'm sure it won't."

Luke smiled at her.

He thought:

"Our Dr. Thomas is in luck!"

"There are people," he said, "who can make the most exciting subject unbearably boring. I'm afraid I'm one of them."

"Oh, but why should you be?"

"I don't know. But the conviction is growing upon me."

Rose Humbleby said:

"You might be one of the people who make dull subjects sound frightfully exciting!"

"Now that *is* a nice thought," said Luke. "Thank you for it."

Rose Humbleby smiled back. Then she said:

"Do you believe in—in superstitions and all that?"

"That's a difficult question. It doesn't follow, you know. One can be interested in things one doesn't believe in."

"Yes, I suppose so," the girl sounded doubtful.

"Are you superstitious?"

"N-no—I don't think so. But I do think things come in —in waves."

"Waves?"

"Waves of bad luck and good luck. I mean—I feel as though lately all Wychwood was under a spell of—of misfortune. Father dying—and Miss Pinkerton being run over, and that little boy who fell out of the window. I—I began to feel as though I hated this place—as though I *must* get away!"

Her breath came rather faster. Luke looked at her thoughtfully.

"So you feel like that?"

"Oh! I know it's silly. I suppose really it was poor daddy dying so unexpectedly—it was so horribly sudden." She shivered. "And then Miss Pinkerton. She said——"

The girl paused.

"What did she say? She was a delightful old lady, I thought —very like a rather special aunt of mine."

"Oh, did you know her?" Rose's face lit up. "I was very fond of her and she was devoted to daddy. But I've sometimes wondered if she was what the Scotch call ' fey.' "

"Why?"

"Because—it's so odd—she seemed quite afraid that something was going to happen to daddy. She almost *warned* me. Especially about accidents. And then that day—just before she went up to town—she was so odd in her manner— absolutely in a *dither*. I really do think, Mr. Fitzwilliam, that she was one of those people who have second sight. I think she *knew* that something was going to happen to her. And she must have known that something was going to happen to daddy too. It's—it's rather frightening, that sort of thing!"

She moved a step nearer to him.

"There are times when one can foresee the future," said Luke. "It isn't always supernatural, though."

"No, I suppose it's quite natural really—just a faculty that most people lack. All the same it—worries me——"

"You mustn't worry," said Luke gently. "Remember, it's all behind you now. It's no good going back over the past. It's the future one has to live for."

"I know. But there's more, you see. . . ." Rose hesitated. "There was something—to do with your cousin."

"My cousin? Bridget?"

"Yes. Miss Pinkerton was worried about her in some way. She was always asking me questions. . . . I think she was afraid for her—too."

Luke turned sharply, scanning the hillside. He had an unreasoning sense of fear. Bridget—alone with the man whose hands had that unhealthy hue of greenish decomposing flesh! Fancy—all fancy! Ellsworthy was only a harmless dilettante who played at shopkeeping.

As though reading his thoughts, Rose said:

"Do you like Mr. Ellsworthy?"

"Emphatically no."

"Geoffrey—Dr. Thomas, you know, doesn't like him either."

"And you?"

"Oh, no—I think he's dreadful." She drew a little nearer. "There's a lot of talk about him. I was told that he had some queer ceremony in the Witches' Meadow—a lot of his friends came down from London—frightfully queer-looking people. And Tommy Pierce was a kind of acolyte."

"Tommy Pierce?" said Luke sharply.

"Yes. He had a surplice and a red cassock."

"When was this?"

"Oh, some time ago—I think it was in March."

"Tommy Pierce seems to have been mixed up in everything that ever took place in this village."

Rose said:

"He was frightfully inquisitive. He always had to know what was going on."

" He probably knew a bit too much in the end," said Luke grimly.

Rose accepted the words at their face value.

" He was rather an odious little boy. He liked cutting up wasps and he teased dogs."

" The kind of boy whose decease is hardly to be regretted! "

" No, I suppose not. It was terrible for his mother, though."

" I gather she has five blessings left to console her. She's got a good tongue, that woman."

" She does talk a lot, doesn't she? "

" After buying a few cigarettes from her, I feel I know the full history of every one in the place! "

Rose said ruefully:

" That's the worst of a place like this. Everybody knows everything about everybody else."

" Oh, no," said Luke.

She looked at him inquiringly.

Luke said with significance:

" No one human being knows the full truth about another human being."

Rose's face grew grave. She gave a slight involuntary shiver.

" No," she said slowly. " I suppose that's true."

" Not even one's nearest and dearest," said Luke.

" Not even——" she stopped. " Oh, I suppose you're right —but I wish you wouldn't say frightening things like that, Mr. Fitzwilliam."

" Does it frighten you? "

Slowly she nodded her head.

Then she turned abruptly.

" I must be going now. If—if you have nothing better to do—I mean if you could—do come and see us. Mother would —would like to see you because of your knowing friends of daddy's long ago."

She walked slowly away down the road. Her head was bent a little as though some weight of care or perplexity bowed it down.

Luke stood looking after her. A sudden wave of solicitude swept over him. He felt a longing to shield and protect this girl.

From what? Asking himself the question, he shook his

head with a momentary impatience at himself. It was true that Rose Humbleby had recently lost her father, but she had a mother, and she was engaged to be married to a decidedly attractive young man who was fully adequate to anything in the protection line. Then why should he, Luke Fitzwilliam, be assailed by this protection complex?

Good old sentimentality to the fore again, thought Luke. The protective male! Flourishing in the Victorian era, going strong in the Edwardian, and still showing signs of life despite what our friend Lord Whitfield would call the rush and strain of modern life!

" All the same," he said to himself as he strolled on towards the looming mass of Ashe Ridge, " I like that girl. She's much too good for Thomas—a cool, superior devil like that."

A memory of the doctor's last smile on the doorstep recurred to him. Decidedly smug it had been! Complacent!

The sound of footsteps a little way ahead roused Luke from his slightly irritable meditations. He looked up to see young Mr. Ellsworthy coming down the path from the hillside. His eyes were on the ground and he was smiling to himself. His expression struck Luke disagreeably. Ellsworthy was not so much walking as prancing—like a man who keeps time to some devilish little jig running in his brain. His smile was a strange secret contortion of the lips—it had a gleeful slyness that was definitely unpleasant.

Luke had stopped, and Ellsworthy was nearly abreast of him when he at last looked up. His eyes, malicious and dancing, met the other man's for just a minute before recognition came. Then, or so it seemed to Luke, a complete change came over the man. Where a minute before there had been the suggestion of a dancing satyr, there was now a somewhat effeminate and priggish young man.

" Oh, Mr. Fitzwilliam, good-morning."

" Good-morning," said Luke. " Have you been admiring the beauties of Nature?"

Mr. Ellsworthy's long, pale hands flew up in a reproving gesture.

" Oh, no, no—oh, dear me, no. I abhor Nature. Such a coarse, unimaginative wench. I have always held that one cannot enjoy life until one has put Nature in her place."

" And how do you propose to do that?"

"There are ways!" said Mr. Ellsworthy. "In a place like this, a delicious provincial spot, there are some most delectable amusements if one has the *goût*—the flair. I enjoy life, Mr. Fitzwilliam."

" So do I," said Luke.

" *Mens sana in corpore sano,*" said Mr. Ellsworthy. His tone was delicately ironic. " I'm sure that's *so* true of you."

"There are worse things," said Luke.

" My dear fellow! Sanity is the one unbelievable bore. One must be mad—deliciously mad—perverted—slightly twisted—then one sees life from a new and entrancing angle."

"The leper's squint," suggested Luke.

" Ah, very good—very good—quite witty! But there's something in it, you know. An interesting angle of vision. But I mustn't detain you. You're having exercise—one must have exercise—the public school spirit!"

" As you say," said Luke, and with a curt nod walked on.

He thought:

" I'm getting too darned imaginative. The fellow's just an ass, that's all."

But some indefinable uneasiness drove his feet on faster. That queer, sly, triumphant smile that Ellsworthy had had on his face—was that just imagination on his, Luke's part? And his subsequent impression that it had been wiped off as though by a sponge the moment the other man caught sight of Luke coming towards him—what of that?

And with quickening uneasiness he thought:

" Bridget? Is she all right? They came up here together and he came back alone."

He hurried on. The sun had come out while he was talking to Rose Humbleby. Now it had gone in again. The sky was dull and menacing, and wind came in sudden erratic little puffs. It was as though he had stepped out of normal everyday life into that queer half-world of enchantment, the consciousness of which had enveloped him ever since he came to Wychwood.

He turned a corner and came out on the flat ledge of green grass that had been pointed out to him from below and which went, he knew, by the name of the Witches' Meadow. It was here, so tradition had it, that the witches had held revelry on Walpurgis Night and Hallowe'en.

And then a quick wave of relief swept over him. Bridget was here. She sat with her back against a rock on the hillside. She was sitting bent over, her head in her hands.

He walked quickly over to her. Lovely springing turf strangely green and fresh.

He said:

" Bridget?"

Slowly she raised her face from her hands. Her face troubled him. She looked as though she were returning from some far-off world, as though she had difficulty in adjusting herself to the world of now and here.

Luke said—rather inadequately:

" I say—you're—you're all right, aren't you?"

It was a minute or two before she answered—as though she still had not quite come back from that far-off world that had held her. Luke felt that his words had to travel a long way before they reached her.

Then she said:

" Of course I'm all right. Why shouldn't I be?"

And now her voice was sharp and almost hostile.

Luke grinned.

" I'm hanged if I know. I got the wind up about you suddenly."

" Why?"

" Mainly, I think, because of the melodramatic atmosphere in which I'm living at present. It makes me see things out of all proportion. If I lose sight of you for an hour or two I naturally assume that the next thing will be to find your gory corpse in a ditch. It would be in a play or a book."

" Heroines are never killed," said Bridget.

" No, but——"

Luke stopped—just in time.

" What were you going to say?"

" Nothing."

Thank goodness he had just stopped himself in time. One couldn't very well say to an attractive young woman, " But you're not the heroine."

Bridget went on:

"They are abducted, imprisoned, left to die of sewer gas or be drowned in cellars—they are always in danger, but they don't ever die."

"Nor even fade away," said Luke.

He went on:

"So this is the Witches' Meadow?"

"Yes."

He looked down at her.

"You only need a broomstick," he said kindly.

"Thank you. Mr. Ellsworthy said much the same."

"I met him just now," said Luke.

"Did you talk to him at all?"

"Yes. I think he tried to annoy me."

"Did he succeed?"

"His methods were rather childish." He paused and then went on abruptly. "He's an odd sort of fellow. One minute you think he's just a mess—and then suddenly one wonders if there isn't a bit more to it than that."

Bridget looked up at him.

"You've felt that too?"

"You agree then?"

"Yes."

Luke waited.

Bridget said:

"There's something—odd about him. I've been wondering, you know. . . . I lay awake last night racking my brains. About the whole business. It seemed to me that if there was a—a killer about, *I* ought to know who it was! I mean, living down here and all that. I thought and I thought and it came to this—if there *is* a killer, he *must* definitely be mad."

Thinking of what Dr. Thomas had said, Luke asked:

"You don't think that a murderer can be as sane as you or I?"

"Not this kind of a murderer. As I see it, this murderer *must* be crazy. And that, you see, brought me straight to Ellsworthy. Of all the people down here, he's the only one who is definitely queer. He *is* queer, you can't get away from it!"

Luke said doubtfully:

"There are a good many of his sort, dilettanti, poseurs—usually quite harmless."

" Yes. But I think there might be a little more than that. He's got such nasty hands."

" You noticed that? Funny, I did too!"

" They're not just white—they're green."

" They do give one that effect. All the same, you can't convict a man of being a murderer because of the colour of his flesh tints."

" Oh, quite. What we want is evidence."

" Evidence!" growled Luke. " Just the one thing that's absolutely lacking. The man's been too careful. A *careful* murderer! A *careful* lunatic!"

" I've been trying to help," said Bridget.

" With Ellsworthy, you mean?"

" Yes. I thought I could probably tackle him better than you could. I've made a beginning."

" Tell me."

" Well, it seems that he has a kind of little coterie—a band of nasty friends. They come down here from time to time and celebrate."

" Do you mean what are called nameless orgies?"

" I don't know about nameless, but certainly orgies. Actually it all sounds very silly and childish."

" I suppose they worship the devil and do obscene dances."

" Something of the kind. Apparently they get a kick out of it."

" I can contribute something to this," said Luke. " Tommy Pierce took part in one of their ceremonies. He was an acolyte. He had a red cassock."

" So he knew about it?"

" Yes. And that might explain his death."

" You mean he talked about it?"

" Yes—or he may have tried a spot of quiet blackmail."

Bridget said thoughtfully:

" I know it's all fantastic—but it doesn't seem quite so fantastic when applied to Ellsworthy as it does to any one else."

" No, I agree—the thing becomes just conceivable instead of being ludicrously unreal."

" We've got a connection with two of the victims," said Bridget. " Tommy Pierce and Amy Gibbs."

" Where do the publican and Humbleby come in?"

" At the moment they don't."

" Not the publican. But I can imagine a motive for Humbleby's removal. He was a doctor and he may have tumbled to Ellsworthy's abnormal state."

" Yes, that's possible."

Then Bridget laughed.

" I did my stuff pretty well this morning. My psychic possibilities are grand, it seems, and when I told how one of my great-great-grandmothers had a near escape of being burnt for witchcraft my stock went soaring up. I rather think that I shall be invited to take part in the orgies at the next meeting of the Satanic Games whenever that may be."

Luke said:

" Bridget, for God's sake, be careful."

She looked at him surprised. He got up.

" I met Humbleby's daughter just now. We were talking about Miss Pinkerton. And the Humbleby girl said that Miss Pinkerton had been worried about you."

Bridget, in the act of rising, stopped as though frozen into immobility.

" What's that? Miss Pinkerton—worried—about *me*?"

" That's what Rose Humbleby said."

" Rose Humbleby said that?"

" Yes."

" What more did she say?"

" Nothing more."

" Are you sure?"

" Quite sure."

There was a pause, then Bridget said, " I see."

" Miss Pinkerton was worried about Humbleby and *he* died. Now I hear she was worried about *you*——"

Bridget laughed. She stood up and shook her head so that her long black hair flew out round her head.

" Don't worry," she said. " The devil looks after his own."

CHAPTER ELEVEN

Domestic Life of Major Horton

LUKE LEANED back in his chair on the other side of the bank manager's table.

"Well, that seems very satisfactory," he said. "I'm afraid I've been taking up a lot of your time."

Mr. Jones waved a deprecating hand. His small, dark, plump face wore a happy expression.

"No, indeed, Mr. Fitzwilliam. This is a quiet spot, you know. We are always glad to see a stranger."

"It's a fascinating part of the world," said Luke. "Full of superstitions."

Mr. Jones sighed and said it took a long time for education to eradicate superstition. Luke remarked that he thought education was too highly rated nowadays and Mr. Jones was slightly shocked by the statement.

"Lord Whitfield," he said, "has been a handsome benefactor here. He realises the disadvantages under which he himself suffered as a boy and is determined that the youth of to-day shall be better equipped."

"Early disadvantages haven't prevented him from making a large fortune," said Luke.

"No, he must have had ability—great ability."

"Or luck," said Luke.

Mr. Jones looked rather shocked.

"Luck is the one thing that counts," said Luke. "Take a murderer, for example. Why does the successful murderer get away with it? Is it ability? Or is it sheer luck?"

Mr. Jones admitted that it was probably luck.

Luke continued:

"Take a fellow like this man Carter, the landlord of one of your pubs. The fellow was probably drunk six nights out of seven—yet one night he goes and pitches himself off the foot-bridge into the river. Luck again."

"Good luck for some people," said the bank manager.

" You mean?"

" For his wife and daughter."

" Oh, yes, of course."

A clerk knocked and entered bearing papers. Luke gave two specimen signatures and was given a cheque-book. He rose.

" Well, I'm glad that's all fixed up. Had a bit of luck over the Derby this year. Did you?"

Mr. Jones said smilingly that he was not a betting man. He added that Mrs. Jones held very strong views on the subject of horse-racing.

" Then I suppose you didn't go to the Derby?"

" No indeed."

" Anybody go to it from here?"

"Major Horton did. He's quite a keen racing man. And Mr. Abbot usually takes the day off. He didn't back the winner, though."

"I don't suppose many people did," said Luke, and departed after the exchange of farewells.

He lit a cigarette as he emerged from the bank. Apart from the theory of the " least likely person," he saw no reason for retaining Mr. Jones on his list of suspects. The bank manager had shown no interesting reactions to Luke's test questions. It seemed quite impossible to visualise him as a murderer. Moreover, he had not been absent on Derby Day. Incidentally, Luke's visit had not been wasted, he had received two small items of information. Both Major Horton and Mr. Abbot, the solicitor, had been away from Wychwood on Derby Day. Either of them, therefore, could have been in London at the time when Miss Pinkerton was run down by a car.

Although Luke did not now suspect Dr. Thomas he felt he would be more satisfied if he knew for a fact that the latter had been at Wychwood engaged in his professional duties on that particular day. He made a mental note to verify that point.

Then there was Ellsworthy. Had Ellsworthy been in Wychwood on Derby Day? If he had, the presumption that he was the killer was correspondingly weakened. Although, Luke noted, it was possible that Miss Pinkerton's death had been neither more nor less than the accident that it was supposed to be.

But he rejected that theory. Her death was too opportune.

Luke got into his own car, which was standing by the kerb, and drove in it to Pipwell's Garage, situated at the far end of the High Street.

There were various small matters in the car's running that he wanted to discuss. A good-looking young mechanic with a freckled face listened intelligently. The two men lifted the bonnet and became absorbed in a technical discussion.

A voice called:

" Jim, come here a minute."

The freckled-faced mechanic obeyed.

Jim Harvey. That was right. Jim Harvey, Amy Gibbs's young man. He returned presently, apologising, and the conversation became technical once more. Luke agreed to leave the car there.

As he was about to leave he inquired casually:

" Do any good on the Derby this year?"

" No, sir. Backed Clarigold."

" Can't be many people who backed Jujube the II.?"

" No, indeed, sir. I don't believe any of the papers even tipped it as an outside chance."

Luke shook his head.

" Racing's an uncertain game. Ever seen the Derby run?"

" No, sir, wish I had. Asked for a day off this year. There was a cheap ticket up to town and down to Epsom, but the boss wouldn't hear of it. We were short-handed, as a matter of fact, and had a lot of work in that day."

Luke nodded and took his departure.

Jim Harvey was crossed off his list. That pleasant-faced boy was not a secret killer, and it was not he who had run down Lavinia Pinkerton.

He strolled home by way of the river bank. Here, as once before, he encountered Major Horton and his dogs. The major was still in the same condition of apoplectic shouting. " Augustus—Nelly—NELLY, I say. Nero—Nero—NERO."

Again the protuberant eyes stared at Luke. But this time there was more to follow. Major Horton said:

"Excuse me. Mr. Fitzwilliam, isn't it?"

"Yes."

"Horton here—Major Horton. Believe I'm going to meet you to-morrow up at the Manor. Tennis party. Miss Conway very kindly asked me. Cousin of yours, isn't she?"

"Yes."

"Thought so. Soon spot a new face down here, you know."

Here a diversion occurred, the three bulldogs advancing upon a nondescript white mongrel.

"Augustus—Nero. Come here, sir—come here, I say."

When Augustus and Nero had finally reluctantly obeyed the command, Major Horton returned to the conversation. Luke was patting Nelly, who was gazing up at him sentimentally.

"Nice bitch, that, isn't she?" said the major. "I like bull-dogs. I've always had 'em. Prefer 'em to any other breed. My place is just near here, come in and have a drink."

Luke accepted and the two men walked together while Major Horton held forth on the subject of dogs and the in-feriority of all other breeds to that which he himself preferred.

Luke heard of the prizes Nelly had won, of the infamous conduct of a judge in awarding Augustus merely a Highly Commended, and of the triumphs of Nero in the show ring.

By then they had turned in at the major's gate. He opened the front door, which was not locked, and the two men passed into the house. Leading the way into a small slightly doggy-smelling room lined with bookshelves, Major Horton busied himself with the drinks. Luke looked round him. There were photographs of dogs, copies of the *Field* and *Country Life* and a couple of well-worn arm-chairs. Silver cups were arranged round the bookcases. There was one oil painting over the mantelpiece.

"My wife," said the major, looking up from the siphon and noting the direction of Luke's glance. "Remarkable woman. A lot of character in her face, don't you think?"

"Yes, indeed," said Luke, looking at the late Mrs. Horton. She was represented in a pink satin dress and was holding a bunch of lilies of the valley. Her brown hair was parted in the middle and her lips were pressed grimly together. Her eyes, of a cold grey, looked out ill-temperedly at the beholder.

"A remarkable woman," said the major, handing a glass to

Luke. " She died over a year ago. I haven't been the same man since."

" No?" said Luke, a little at a loss to know what to say.

" Sit down," said the major, waving a hand towards one of the leather chairs.

He himself took the other one and sipping his whisky and soda, he went on:

" No, I haven't been the same man since."

" You must miss her," said Luke awkwardly.

Major Horton shook his head darkly.

" Fellow needs a wife to keep him up to scratch," he said. " Otherwise he gets slack—yes, slack. He lets himself go."

" But surely——"

" My boy, I know what I'm talking about. Mind you, I'm not saying marriage doesn't come hard on a fellow at first. It does. Fellow says to himself, damn it all, he says, I can't call my soul my own! But he gets broken in. It's all discipline."

Luke thought that Major Horton's married life must have been more like a military campaign than an idyll of domestic bliss.

" Women," soliloquised the major " are a rum lot. It seems sometimes that there's no pleasing them. But by Jove, they keep a man up to the mark."

Luke preserved a respectful silence.

" You married?" inquired the major.

" No."

" Ah, well, you'll come to it. And mind you, my boy, there's nothing like it."

" It's always cheering," said Luke, " to hear some one speak well of the marriage state. Especially in these days of easy divorce."

" Pah!" said the major. " Young people make me sick. No stamina—no endurance. They can't stand anything. No *fortitude*!"

Luke itched to ask why such exceptional fortitude should be needed, but he controlled himself.

" Mind you," said the major, " Lydia was a woman in a thousand—in a thousand! Every one here respected and looked up to her."

" Yes?"

" She wouldn't stand any nonsense. She'd got a way of fixing a person with her eye—and the person wilted—just wilted. Some of these half-baked girls who call themselves servants nowadays. They think you'll put up with any insolence. Lydia soon showed them! Do you know we had fifteen cooks and house-parlourmaids in one year. *Fifteen!*"

Luke felt that this was hardly a tribute to Mrs. Horton's domestic management, but since it seemed to strike his host differently he merely murmured some vague remark.

" Turned 'em out neck and crop, she did, if they didn't suit."

" Was it always that way about?" asked Luke.

" Well, of course a lot of them walked out on us. A good riddance—that's what Lydia used to say!"

" A fine spirit," said Luke, " but wasn't it sometimes rather awkward?"

" Oh! I didn't mind turning to and putting my hand to things," said Horton. " I'm a pretty fair cook and I can lay a fire with any one. I've never cared for washing up but of course it's got to be done—you can't get away from that."

Luke agreed that you couldn't. He asked whether Mrs. Horton had been good at domestic work.

" I'm not the sort of fellow to let his wife wait on him," said Major Horton. " And anyway Lydia was far too delicate to do any housework."

" She wasn't strong then?"

Major Horton shook his head.

" She had wonderful spirit. She wouldn't give in. But what that woman suffered! And no sympathy from the doctors either. Doctors are callous brutes. They only understand downright physical pain. Anything out of the ordinary is beyond most of them. Humbleby, for instance, every one seemed to *think* he was a good doctor."

" You don't agree."

" The man was an absolute ignoramus. Knew nothing of modern discoveries. Doubt if he'd ever heard of a neurosis! He understood measles and mumps and broken bones all right, I suppose. But nothing else. Had a row with him in the end. He didn't understand Lydia's case at all. I gave it him straight from the shoulder and he didn't like it. Got huffed and backed right out. Said I could send for any other doctor I chose. After that, we had Thomas."

"You liked him better?"

"Altogether a much cleverer man. If any one could have pulled her through her last illness Thomas would have done it. As a matter of fact she was getting better, but she had a sudden relapse."

"Was it painful?"

"H'm, yes. Gastritis. Acute pain—sickness—all the rest of it. How that poor woman suffered! She was a martyr if there ever was one. And a couple of hospital nurses in the house who were about as sympathetic as a brace of grandfather clocks! 'The patient this' and 'the patient that.'" The major shook his head and drained his glass. "Can't stand hospital nurses! So smug. Lydia insisted they were poisoning her. That wasn't true, of course—a regular sick fancy—lots of people have it, so Thomas said—but there was this much truth behind it—those women disliked her. That's the worst of women—always down on their own sex."

"I suppose," said Luke feeling that he was putting it awkwardly but not seeing how to put it better, "that Mrs. Horton had a lot of devoted friends in Wychwood?"

"People were very kind," said the major somewhat grudgingly. "Whitfield sent down grapes and peaches from his hot-house. And the old tabbies used to come and sit with her. Honoria Waynflete and Lavinia Pinkerton."

"Miss Pinkerton came often, did she?"

"Yes. Regular old maid—but a kind creature! Very worried about Lydia she was. Used to inquire into the diet and the medicines. All kindly meant, you know, but what I call a lot of *fuss*."

Luke nodded comprehendingly.

"Can't stand fuss," said the major. "Too many women in this place. Difficult to get a decent game of golf."

"What about the young fellow at the antique shop?" said Luke.

The major snorted:

"He doesn't play golf. Much too much of a Miss Nancy."

"Has he been in Wychwood long?"

" About two years. Nasty sort of fellow. Hate those long-haired purring chaps. Funnily enough Lydia liked him. You can't trust women's judgment about men. They cotton to some amazing bounders. She even insisted on taking some patent quack nostrum of his. Stuff in a purple glass jar with signs of the Zodiac all over it! Supposed to be certain herbs picked at the full of the moon. Lot of tomfoolery, but women swallow that stuff—swallow it literally too—ha, ha ! "

Luke said, feeling that he was changing the subject rather abruptly, but correctly judging that Major Horton would not be aware of the fact :

" What sort of fellow is Abbot, the local solicitor? Pretty sound on the law? I've got to have some legal advice about something and I thought I might go to him."

" They say he's pretty shrewd," acknowledged Major Horton. " I don't know. Matter of fact I've had a row with him. Not seen him since he came out here to make Lydia's will for her just before she died. In my opinion the man's a cad. But of course," he added. " that doesn't affect his ability as a lawyer."

" No, of course not," said Luke. " He seems a quarrelsome sort of man, though. Seems to have fallen out with a good many people from what I hear."

" Trouble with him is that he's so confoundedly touchy," said Major Horton. " Seems to think he's God Almighty and that any one who disagrees with him is committing *lèse-majesté*. Heard of his row with Humbleby?"

" They had a row, did they?"

" First-class row. Mind you, that doesn't surprise me. Humbleby was an opinionated ass! Still, there it is."

" His death was very sad."

" Humbleby's? Yes, I suppose it was. Lack of ordinary care. Blood poisoning's a damned dangerous thing. Always put iodine on a cut—I do! Simple precaution. Humbleby, who's a doctor, doesn't do anything of the sort. It just shows."

Luke was not quite sure what it showed, but he let that pass. Glancing at his watch he got up.

Major Horton said :

" Getting on for lunch time? So it is. Well, glad to have had a chat with you. Does me good to see a man who's been about the world a bit. We must have a yarn some other time.

Where was your show? Mayang Straits? Never been there. Hear you're writing a book. Superstitions and all that."

" Yes—I——"

But Major Horton swept on.

" I can tell you several very interesting things. When I was in India, my boy——"

Luke escaped some ten minutes later after enduring the usual histories of fakirs, rope and mango tricks, dear to the retired Anglo-Indian.

As he stepped out into the open air, and heard the Major's voice bellowing to Nero behind him, he marvelled at the miracle of married life. Major Horton seemed genuinely to regret a wife whom by all accounts, not excluding his own, must have been nearly allied to a man-eating tiger.

Or was it—Luke asked himself the question suddenly— was it an exceedingly clever bluff?

CHAPTER TWELVE

Passage of Arms

THE AFTERNOON of the tennis party was fortunately fine. Lord Whitfield was in his most genial mood, acting the part of the host with a good deal of enjoyment. He referred frequently to his humble origin. The players were eight in all. Lord Whitfield, Bridget, Luke, Rose Humbleby, Mr. Abbot, Dr. Thomas, Major Horton and Hetty Jones, a giggling young woman who was the daughter of the bank manager.

In the second set of the afternoon, Luke found himself partnering Bridget against Lord Whitfield and Rose Humbleby. Rose was a good player with a strong forehand drive and played in county matches. She atoned for Lord Whitfield's failures, and Bridget and Luke who were neither of them particularly strong, made quite an even match of it. They were three games all, and then Luke found a streak of erratic brilliance and he and Bridget forged ahead to five—three.

It was then he observed that Lord Whitfield was losing his temper. He argued over a line ball, declared a serve to be

a fault in spite of Rose's disclaimer, and displayed all the
attributes of a peevish child. It was set point, but Bridget sent
an easy shot into the net and immediately after served a double
fault. Deuce. The next ball was returned down the middle
line and as he prepared to take it he and his partner collided.
Then Bridget served another double fault and the game was
lost.

Bridget apologised. "Sorry, I've gone to pieces."

It seemed true enough. Bridget's shots were wild and she
seemed to be unable to do anything right. The set ended with
Lord Whitfield and his partner victorious at the score of
eight—six.

There was a momentary discussion as to the composition
of the next set. In the end Rose played again with Mr. Abbot
as her partner against Dr. Thomas and Miss Jones.

Lord Whitfield sat down, wiping his forehead and smiling
complacently, his good humour quite restored. He began to
talk to Major Horton on the subject of a series of articles on
Fitness for Britain which one of his papers was starring.

Luke said to Bridget:

"Show me the kitchen garden."

"Why the kitchen garden?"

"I have a feeling for cabbages."

"Won't green peas do?"

"Green peas would be admirable."

They walked away from the tennis court and came to the
walled kitchen garden. It was empty of gardeners this Saturday afternoon and looked lazy and peaceful in the sunshine.

"Here are your peas," said Bridget.

Luke paid no attention to the object of the visit. He said:

"Why the hell did you give them the set?"

Bridget's eyebrows went up a fraction.

"I'm sorry. I went to bits. My tennis is erratic."

"Not so erratic as that! Those double faults of yours
wouldn't deceive a child! And those wild shots—each of them
half a mile out!"

Bridget said calmly:

"That's because I'm such a rotten tennis player. If I were
a bit better I could perhaps have made it a bit more plausible!"

But as it is if I try to make a ball go just out, it's always on the line and all the good work still to do."

" Oh, you admit it then?"

" Obvious, my dear Watson."

" And the reason?"

" Equally obvious, I should have thought. Gordon doesn't like losing."

" And what about me? Supposing I like to win?"

" I'm afraid, my dear Luke, that that isn't equally important."

" Would you like to make your meaning just a little clearer still?"

" Certainly, if you like. One mustn't quarrel with one's bread and butter. Gordon is my bread and butter. You are not."

Luke drew a deep breath. Then he exploded.

" What the hell do you mean by marrying that absurd little man? Why are you doing it?"

" Because as his secretary I get six pounds a week, and as his wife I shall get a hundred thousand settled on me, a jewel-case full of pearls and diamonds, a handsome allowance, and various perquisites of the married state!"

" But for somewhat different duties!"

Bridget said coldly:

" *Must* we have this melodramatic attitude towards every single thing in life? If you are contemplating a pretty picture of Gordon as an uxorious husband, you can wash it right out! Gordon, as you should have realised, is a small boy who has not quite grown up. What he needs is a mother, not a wife. Unfortunately his mother died when he was four years old. What he wants is some one at hand to whom he can brag, some one who will reassure him about himself and who is pre-pared to listen indefinitely to Lord Whitfield on the subject of Himself!"

" You've got a bitter tongue, haven't you?"

Bridget retorted sharply:

" I don't tell myself fairy stories if that's what you mean! I'm a young woman with a certain amount of intelligence, very moderate looks, and no money. I intend to earn an honest living. My job as Gordon's wife will be practically indistinguishable from my job as Gordon's secretary. After a year I doubt if he'll remember to kiss me good-night. The only difference is in the salary."

They looked at each other. Both of them were pale with anger. Bridget said jeeringly:

"Go on. You're rather old-fashioned, aren't you, Mr. Fitzwilliam. Hadn't you better trot out the old *clichés*—say that I'm selling myself for money—that's always a good one, I think!"

Luke said: "You're a cold-blooded little devil!"

"That's better than being a hot-blooded little fool!"

"Is it?"

"Yes. I know."

Luke sneered. "What do you know?"

"I know what it is to care about a man! Did you ever meet Johnnie Cornish? I was engaged to him for three years. He was adorable—I cared like hell about him—cared so much that it *hurt*! Well, he threw me over and married a nice plump widow with a North-Country accent and three chins and an income of thirty thousand a year! That sort of thing rather cures one of romance, don't you think?"

Luke turned away with a sudden groan. He said:

"It might."

"It did. . . ."

There was a pause. The silence lay heavy between them. Bridget broke it at last. She said, but with a slight uncertainty in her tone:

"I hope you realise that you had no earthly right to speak to me as you did. You're staying in Gordon's house and it's damned bad taste!"

Luke recovered his composure.

"Isn't that rather a *cliché* too?" he inquired politely.

Bridget flushed. "It's true, anyway!"

"It isn't. I had every right."

"Nonsense!"

Luke looked at her. His face had a queer pallor, like a man who is suffering physical pain. He said:

"I *have* a right. I've the right of caring for you—what did you say just now?—of caring so much that it hurts!"

She drew back a step. She said: " You——"

" Yes, funny, isn't it? The sort of thing that ought to give you a hearty laugh! I came down here to do a job of work and *you* came round the corner of that house and—how can I say it—put a spell on me! That's what it feels like. You mentioned fairy stories just now. I'm caught up in a fairy story! You've bewitched me. I've a feeling that if you pointed your finger at me and said: 'Turn into a frog,' I'd go hopping away with my eyes popping out of my head."

He took a step nearer to her.

" I love you like hell, Bridget Conway. And, loving you like hell, you can't expect me to enjoy seeing you get married to a pot-bellied pompous little peer who loses his temper when he doesn't win at tennis."

" What do you suggest I should do?"

" I suggest that you should marry me instead! But doubtless that suggestion will give rise to a lot of merry laughter."

" The laughter is positively uproarious."

" Exactly. Well, now we know where we are. Shall we return to the tennis court? Perhaps this time you will find me a partner who can play to win!"

" Really," said Bridget sweetly, " I believe you mind losing just as much as Gordon does!"

Luke caught her suddenly by the shoulders.

" You've got a devilish tongue, haven't you, Bridget?"

" I'm afraid you don't like me very much, Luke, however great your passion for me!"

" I don't think I like you at all."

Bridget said, watching him:

" You meant to get married and settle down when you came home, didn't you?"

" Yes."

" But not to some one like me?"

" I never thought of any one in the least like you."

" No—you wouldn't—I know your type. I know it exactly."

" You are so clever, dear Bridget."

" A really nice girl—thoroughly English—fond of the country and good with dogs. . . . You probably visualised her in a tweed skirt stirring a log fire with the tip of her shoe."

" The picture sounds most attractive."

" I'm sure it does. Shall we return to the tennis court? You can play with Rose Humbleby. She's so good that you're practically certain to win."

" Being old-fashioned I must allow you to have the last word."

Again there was a pause. Then Luke took his hands slowly from her shoulders. They both stood uncertain as though something still unsaid lingered between them.

Then Bridget turned abruptly and led the way back. The next set was just ending. Rose protested against playing again.

" I've played two sets running."

Bridget, however, insisted.

" I'm feeling tired. I don't want to play. You and Mr. Fitzwilliam take on Miss Jones and Major Horton."

But Rose continued to protest and in the end a men's four was arranged. Afterwards came tea.

Lord Whitfield conversed with Dr. Thomas, describing at length and with great self-importance a visit he had recently paid to the Wellerman Kreitz Research Laboratories.

" I wanted to understand the trend of the latest scientific discoveries for myself," he explained earnestly. " I'm responsible for what my papers print. I feel that very keenly. This is a scientific age. Science must be made easily assimilable by the masses."

" A little science might possibly be a dangerous thing," said Dr. Thomas with a slight shrug of his shoulders.

" Science in the home, that's what we have to aim at," said Lord Whitfield. " Science minded——"

" Test tube conscious," said Bridget gravely.

" I was impressed," said Lord Whitfield. " Wellerman took me round himself, of course. I begged him to leave me to an underling, but he insisted."

" Naturally," said Luke.

Lord Whitfield looked gratified.

" And he explained everything most clearly—the culture—the serum—the whole principle of the thing. He agreed to contribute the first article in the series himself."

Mrs. Anstruther murmured:

"They use guinea-pigs, I believe—so cruel—though of course not so bad as dogs—or even cats."

"Fellows who use dogs ought to be shot," said Major Horton, hoarsely.

"I really believe, Horton," said Mr. Abbot, "that you value canine life above human life."

"Every time!" said the major. "Dogs can't turn round on you like human beings can. Never get a nasty word from a dog."

"Only a nasty tooth stuck into your leg," said Mr. Abbot. "Eh, Horton?"

"Dogs are a good judge of character," said Major Horton,

"One of your brutes nearly pinned me by the leg last week. What do you say to that, Horton?"

"Same as I said just now!"

Bridget interposed tactfully:

"What about some more tennis?"

A couple more sets were played. Then, as Rose Humbleby said good-bye, Luke appeared beside her.

"I'll see you home," he said. "And carry the tennis bat. You haven't got a car, have you?"

"No, but it's no distance."

"I'd like a walk."

He said no more, merely taking her racquet and shoes from her. They walked down the drive without speaking. Then Rose mentioned one or two trivial matters. Luke answered rather shortly but the girl did not seem to notice.

As they turned into the gate of her house, Luke's face cleared.

"I'm feeling better now," he said.

"Were you feeling badly before?"

"Nice of you to pretend you didn't notice it. You've exorcised the brute's sulky temper, though. Funny, I feel as though I'd come out of a dark cloud into the sun."

"So you have. There was a cloud over the sun when we left the Manor and now it's passed over."

"So it's literally as well as figuratively. Well, well—the world's a good place after all."

"Of course it is."

"Miss Humbleby, may I be impertinent?"

" I'm sure you couldn't be."

" Oh, don't be too sure of that. I wanted to say that I think Dr. Thomas is a very lucky man."

Rose blushed and smiled.

She said: " So you've heard?"

" Was it supposed to be a secret? I'm so sorry."

" Oh! Nothing is a secret in this place," said Rose ruefully.

" So it is true—you and he are engaged?"

Rose nodded.

" Only—just now—we're not announcing it officially. You see, daddy was against it and it seems—well—unkind to—to blazon it abroad the moment he's dead."

" Your father disapproved?"

" Well, not *disapproved* exactly. Oh, I suppose it did amount to that, really."

Luke said gently:

" He thought you were too young?"

" That's what he said."

Luke said acutely: " But you think there was something more than that?"

Rose bent her head slowly and reluctantly.

" Yes—I'm afraid what it really amounted to was that daddy didn't—well, didn't really *like* Geoffrey."

" They were antagonistic to each other?"

" It seemed like that sometimes. . . . Of course, daddy was rather a prejudiced old dear."

" And I suppose he was very fond of you and didn't like the thought of losing you?"

Rose assented but still with a shade of reservation in her manner.

" It went deeper than that?" asked Luke. " He definitely didn't want Thomas as a husband for you?"

" No. You see—daddy and Geoffrey are so very unlike— and in some ways they clashed. Geoffrey was really very patient and good about it—but knowing daddy didn't like him made him even more reserved and shy in his manner, so that daddy really never got to know him any better."

" Prejudices are very hard to combat," said Luke.

" It was so completely unreasonable!"

" Your father didn't advance any reasons?"

"Oh, no. He couldn't! Naturally, I mean, there wasn't anything he could say against Geoffrey except that he didn't like him."

"*I do not like thee, Dr. Fell, the reason why I cannot tell.*"

"Exactly."

"No tangible thing to get hold of? I mean, your Geoffrey doesn't drink or back horses?"

"Oh, no. I don't believe Geoffrey even knows what won the Derby."

"That's funny," said Luke. "You know, I could swear I saw your Dr. Thomas at Epsom on Derby Day."

For a moment he was anxious lest he might already have mentioned that he only arrived in England on that day. But Rose responded at once quite unsuspiciously.

"You thought you saw Geoffrey at the Derby? Oh, no. He couldn't get away, for one thing. He was over at Ashewold nearly all that day at a difficult confinement case."

"What a memory you've got!"

Rose laughed.

"I remember that, because he told me they called the baby Jujube as a nickname!"

Luke nodded abstractly.

"Anyway," said Rose, "Geoffrey never goes to race meetings. He'd be bored to death."

She added, in a different tone:

"Won't you—come in? I think mother would like to see you."

"If you're sure of that?"

Rose led the way into a room where twilight hung rather sadly. A woman was sitting in an armchair in a curiously huddled up position.

"Mother, this is Mr. Fitzwilliam."

Mrs. Humbleby gave a start and shook hands. Rose went quietly out of the room.

"I'm glad to see you, Mr. Fitzwilliam. Some friends of yours knew my husband many years ago, so Rose tells me."

"Yes, Mrs. Humbleby." He rather hated repeating the lie to the widowed woman, but there was no way out of it.

Mrs. Humbleby said:

" I wish you could have met him. He was a fine man and a great doctor. He cured many people who had been given up as hopeless just by the strength of his personality."

Luke said gently:

" I've heard a lot about him since I've been here. I know how much people thought of him."

He could not see Mrs. Humbleby's face very distinctly. Her voice was rather monotonous, but its very lack of feeling seemed to emphasise the fact that actually feeling was in her, strenuously held back.

She said rather unexpectedly:

" The world is a very wicked place, Mr. Fitzwilliam. Do you know that?"

Luke was a little surprised.

" Yes, perhaps that may be."

She insisted:

" No, but do you *know* it? It's important that. There's a lot of wickedness about. . . . One must be prepared—to fight it! John was. *He* knew. He was on the side of the right!"

Luke said gently:

" I'm sure he was."

" He knew the wickedness there was in *this* place," said Mrs. Humbleby. " He knew——"

She burst suddenly into tears.

Luke murmured:

" I'm so sorry——" and stopped.

She controlled herself as suddenly as she had lost control.

" You must forgive me," she said. She held out her hand and he took it. " Do come and see us while you are here," she said. " It would be so good for Rose. She likes you so much."

" I like her. I think your daughter is the nicest girl I've met for a long time, Mrs. Humbleby."

" She's very good to me."

" Dr. Thomas is a very lucky man."

" Yes." Mrs. Humbleby dropped his hand. Her voice had gone flat again. " I don't know—it's all so difficult."

Luke left her standing in the half gloom, her fingers nervously twisting and untwisting themselves.

As he walked home his mind went over various aspects of the conversation.

Dr. Thomas had been absent from Wychwood for a good part of Derby Day. He had been absent in a car. Wychwood was thirty-five miles from London. Supposedly he had been attending a confinement case. Was there more than his word? The point, he supposed could be verified. His mind went on to Mrs. Humbleby.

What had she meant by her insistence on that phrase, " *There's a lot of wickedness about . . .*"?

Was she just nervous and overwrought by the shock of her husband's death? Or was there something more to it than that?

Did she perhaps know something? Something that Dr. Humbleby had known before he died?

" I've got to go on with this," said Luke to himself. " I've got to go on."

Resolutely he averted his mind from the passage of arms that had taken place between him and Bridget.

CHAPTER THIRTEEN

Miss Waynflete Talks

ON THE following morning Luke came to a decision. He had, he felt, proceeded as far as he could with indirect inquiries. It was inevitable that sooner or later he would be forced into the open. He felt that the time had come to drop the book-writing camouflage and reveal that he had come to Wychwood with a definite aim in view.

In pursuance of this plan of campaign he decided to call upon Honoria Waynflete. Not only had he been favourably impressed by that middle-aged spinster's air of discretion and a certain shrewdness of outlook—but he fancied that she might have information that would help him. He believed that she had told him what she *knew*. He wanted to induce her to tell him what she might have *guessed*. He had a shrewd idea that Miss Waynflete's guesses might be fairly near the truth.

He called immediately after church.

Miss Waynflete received him in a matter-of-fact manner, showing no surprise at his call. As she sat down near him, her prim hands folded and her intelligent eyes—so like an amiable goat's—fixed on his face, he found little difficulty in coming to the object of his visit.

He said: "I dare say you have guessed, Miss Waynflete, that the reason of my coming here is not merely to write a book on local customs?"

Miss Waynflete inclined her head and continued to listen.

Luke was not minded as yet to go into the full story. Miss Waynflete might be discreet—she certainly gave him the impression of being so—but where an elderly spinster was concerned Luke felt he could hardly rely on her resisting the temptation to confide an exciting story to one or two trusted cronies. He thereupon proposed to adopt a middle course.

"I am down here to inquire into the circumstances of the death of that poor girl, Amy Gibbs."

Miss Waynflete said:

"You mean you have been sent down by the police?"

"Oh, no—I'm not a plain-clothes dick." He added with a slightly humorous inflection, "I'm afraid I'm that well-known character in fiction, the private investigator."

"I see. Then it was Bridget Conway who brought you down here?"

Luke hesitated a moment. Then he decided to let it go at that. Without going into the whole Pinkerton story, it was difficult to account for his presence. Miss Waynflete was continuing, a note of gentle admiration in her voice.

"Bridget is so practical—so efficient! I'm afraid, if it had been left to *me,* I should have distrusted my own judgment—I mean, that if you are not absolutely sure of a thing, it is so difficult to commit yourself to a definite course of action."

"But you are sure, aren't you?"

Miss Waynflete said gravely:

"No, indeed, Mr. Fitzwilliam. It is not a thing one can be sure about! I mean, it *might* all be imagination. Living alone, with no one to consult or to talk to, one might easily become melodramatic and imagine things which had no foundation in fact."

Luke assented readily to this statement, recognising its inherent truth, but he added gently:

"But you are sure in your own mind?"

Even here Miss Waynflete showed a little reluctance.

"We are not talking at cross purposes, I hope?" she demurred.

Luke smiled.

"You would like me to put it in plain words? Very well. You do think that Amy Gibbs was murdered?"

Honoria Waynflete flinched a little at the crudity of the language. She said:

"I don't feel at all happy about her death. Not at all happy. The whole thing is profoundly unsatisfactory in my opinion."

Luke said patiently:

"But you don't think her death was a natural one?"

"No."

"You don't believe it was an accident?"

"It seems to me most improbable. There are so many——"

Luke cut her short.

"You don't think it was suicide?"

"Emphatically not."

"Then," said Luke gently, "you *do* think that it was murder?"

Miss Waynflete hesitated, gulped, and bravely took the plunge.

"Yes," she said. "I do!"

"Good. Now we can get on with things."

"But I have really no *evidence* on which to base that belief," Miss Waynflete explained anxiously. "It is entirely an *idea*!"

"Quite so. This is a private conversation. We are merely speaking about what we *think* and *suspect*. We *suspect* Amy Gibbs was murdered. Who do we *think* murdered her?"

Miss Waynflete shook her head. She was looking very troubled.

Luke said, watching her:

"Who had reason to murder her?"

Miss Waynflete said slowly:

"She had had a quarrel, I believe, with her young man at the garage, Jim Harvey—a most steady, superior young man. I know one reads in the papers of young men attacking their sweethearts and dreadful things like that, but I really can't believe that Jim would do such a thing."

Luke nodded.

Miss Waynflete went on.

"Besides, I can't believe that he would do it that way. Climb up to her window and substitute a bottle of poison for the other one with the cough mixture. I mean, that doesn't seem——"

Luke came to the rescue as she hesitated.

"It's not the act of an angry lover? I agree. In my opinion we can wash Jim Harvey right out. Amy was killed (we're agreeing she *was* killed) by some one who wanted to get her out of the way and who planned the crime carefully so that it should appear to be an accident. Now have you any idea— any *hunch*—shall we put it like that?—who that person could be?"

Miss Waynflete said:

"No—really—no, I haven't the least idea!"

"Sure?"

"N-no—no, indeed."

Luke looked at her thoughtfully. The denial, he felt, had not rung quite true. He went on:

"You know of no motive?"

"No motive whatever."

That was more emphatic.

"Had she been in many places in Wychwood?"

"She was with the Hortons for a year before going to Lord Whitfield."

Luke summed up rapidly.

"It's like this, then. Somebody wanted that girl out of the way. From the given facts we assume that—first—it was a man and a man of moderately old-fashioned outlook (as shown by the hat paint touch), and secondly that it must have been a reasonably athletic man since it is clear he must have climbed up over the outhouse to the girl's window. You agree on those points?"

"Absolutely," said Miss Waynflete.

"Do you mind if I go round and have a try myself?"

"Not at all. I think it is a very good idea."

She led him out by a side door and round to the back yard. Luke managed to reach the outhouse roof without much trouble. From there he could easily raise the sash of the girl's window and with a slight effort hoist himself into the room. A few minutes later he rejoined Miss Waynflete on the path below, wiping his hands on his handkerchief.

"Actually it's easier than it looks," he said. "You want a certain amount of muscle, that's all. There were no signs on the sill or outside?"

Miss Waynflete shook her head.

"I don't think so. Of course the constable climbed up this way."

"So that if there were any traces they would be taken to be his. How the police force assists the criminal! Well, that's that!"

Miss Waynflete led the way back to the house.

"Was Amy Gibbs a heavy sleeper?" he asked.

Miss Waynflete replied acidly:

"It was extremely difficult to get her up in the morning. Sometimes I would knock again and again, and call out to her before she answered. But then, you know, Mr. Fitzwilliam, there's a saying there are none so deaf as those who will not hear!"

"That's true," acknowledged Luke. "Well, now, Miss Waynflete, we come to the question of *motive*. Starting with the most obvious one, do you think there was anything between that fellow Ellsworthy and the girl?" He added hastily, "This is just your *opinion* I'm asking. Only that."

"If it's a matter of opinion, I would say yes."

Luke nodded.

"In your opinion, would the girl Amy have stuck at a spot of blackmail?"

"Again as a matter of opinion, I should say that that was quite possible."

"Do you happen to know if she had much money in her possession at the time of her death?"

Miss Waynflete reflected.

"I do not think so. If she had had any unusual amount I think I should have heard about it."

"And she hadn't launched into any unusual extravagance before she died?"

"I don't think so."

"That rather militates against the blackmail theory. The victim usually pays once before he decides to proceed to extremes. There's another theory. The girl might *know* something."

"What kind of thing?"

"She might have knowledge that was dangerous to some one here in Wychwood. We'll take a strictly hypothetical case. She'd been in service in a good many houses here. Supposing she came to know of something that would damage say, some one like Mr. Abbot, professionally."

"Mr. Abbot?"

Luke said quickly:

"Or possibly some negligence or unprofessional conduct on the part of Dr. Thomas."

Miss Waynflete began, "But surely——" and then stopped.

Luke went on:

"Amy Gibbs was housemaid, you said, in the Hortons' house at the time when Mrs. Horton died."

There was a moment's pause, then Miss Waynflete said:

"Will you tell me, Mr. Fitzwilliam, why you bring the Hortons into this? Mrs. Horton died over a year ago."

"Yes, and the girl Amy was there at the time."

"I see. What have the Hortons to do with it?"

"I don't know. I—just wondered. Mrs. Horton died of acute gastritis, didn't she?"

"Yes."

"Was her death at all unexpected?"

Miss Waynflete said slowly:

"It was to me. You see, she had been getting much better—seemed well on the road to recovery—and then she had a sudden relapse and died."

"Was Dr. Thomas surprised?"

"I don't know. I believe he was."

"And the nurses, what did they say?"

"In my experience," said Miss Waynflete, "hospital nurses

are never surprised at any case taking a turn for the worse!
It is recovery that surprises them."

"But her death surprised you?" Luke persisted.

"Yes. I had been with her only the day before, and she
had seemed very much better, talked and seemed quite cheerful."

"What did she think about her own illness?"

"She complained that the nurses were poisoning her. She
had had one nurse sent away, but she said these two were just
as bad!"

"I suppose you didn't pay much attention to that?"

"Well, no, I thought it was all part of the illness. And
she was a very suspicious woman and—it may be unkind to
say so—but she liked to make herself *important*. No doctor
ever understood her case—and it was never anything simple
—it must either be some very obscure disease or else somebody was ' trying to get her out of the way.' "

Luke tried to make his voice casual.

"She didn't suspect her husband of trying to do her in?"

"Oh, *no*, that idea never occurred to her!"

Miss Waynflete paused a minute, then she asked quietly:
"Is that what you think?"

Luke said slowly:

"Husbands have done that before and got away with it.
Mrs. Horton from all accounts was a woman any man might
have longed to be rid of! And I understand that he came
into a good deal of money on her death."

"Yes, he did."

"What do *you* think, Miss Waynflete?"

"You want my opinion?"

"Yes, just your opinion."

Miss Waynflete said quietly and deliberately:

"In my opinion, Major Horton was quite devoted to his
wife and would never have dreamed of doing such a thing."

Luke looked at her and received the mild amber glance
in reply. It did not waver.

"Well," he said, "I expect you're right. You'd probably
know if it was the other way round."

Miss Waynflete permitted herself a smile.

"We women are good observers, you think?"

" Absolutely first-class. Would Miss Pinkerton have agreed with you, do you think?"

" I don't think I ever heard Lavinia express an opinion."

" What did she think about Amy Gibbs?"

Miss Waynflete frowned a little as though thinking.

" It's difficult to say. Lavinia had a very curious idea."

" What idea?"

" She thought that there was something odd going on here in Wychwood."

" She thought, for instance, that somebody pushed Tommy Pierce out of that window?"

Miss Waynflete stared at him in astonishment.

" How *did* you know that, Mr. Fitzwilliam?"

" She told me so. Not in these words, but she gave me the general idea."

Miss Waynflete leant forward, pink with excitement.

" When was this, Mr. Fitzwilliam?"

Luke said quietly, " The day she was killed. We travelled together to London."

" What did she tell you exactly?"

" She told me that there had been too many deaths in Wychwood. She mentioned Amy Gibbs, and Tommy Pierce and that man Carter. She also said that Dr. Humbleby would be the next to go."

Miss Waynflete nodded slowly.

" Did she tell you who was responsible?"

" A man with a certain look in his eyes," said Luke grimly. " A look you couldn't mistake, according to her. She'd seen that look in his eye when he was talking to Humbleby. That's why she said Humbleby would be the next to go."

" And he was," whispered Miss Waynflete. " Oh, dear. Oh, dear."

She leaned back. Her eyes had a stricken look in them.

" Who was the man?" said Luke. " Come now, Miss Waynflete, you know, you *must* know!"

" I don't. She didn't tell me."

" But you can guess," said Luke keenly. " You've a very shrewd idea of who was in her mind."

Reluctantly Miss Waynflete bowed her head.

" Then tell me."

But Miss Waynflete shook her head energetically.

"No, indeed. You're asking me to do something that is highly improper! You're asking me to *guess* at what may —only *may*, mind you—have been in the mind of a friend *who is now dead*. I couldn't make an accusation of that kind!"

"It wouldn't be an accusation—only an opinion."

But Miss Waynflete was unexpectedly firm.

"I've nothing to go on—nothing whatever," she said. "Lavinia never actually *said* anything to me. I may *think* she had a certain idea—but you see I might be entirely *wrong*. And then I should have misled you and perhaps serious consequences might ensue. It would be very wicked and unfair of me to mention a *name*. And I may be quite, quite wrong! In fact, I probably *am* wrong!"

And Miss Waynflete set her lips firmly and glared at Luke with a grim determination.

Luke knew how to accept defeat when he met it.

He realised that Miss Waynflete's sense of rectitude and something else more nebulous that he could not quite place were both against him.

He accepted defeat with a good grace and rose to say goodbye. He had every intention of returning to the charge later, but he allowed no hint of that to escape into his manner.

"You must do as you think right, of course," he said. "Thank you for the help you have given me."

Miss Waynflete seemed to become a little less sure of herself as she accompanied him to the door.

"I hope you don't think," she began, then changed the form of the sentence. "If there is anything else I can do to help you, please, please let me know."

"I will. You won't repeat this conversation, will you?"

"Of course not. I shan't say a word to anybody."

Luke hoped that that was true.

"Give my love to Bridget," said Miss Waynflete. "She's such a handsome girl, isn't she? And clever too. I—I hope she will be happy."

And as Luke looked a question, she added:

"Married to Lord Whitfield, I mean. Such a great difference in age."

"Yes, there is."

Miss Waynflete sighed.

"You know that I was engaged to him once," she said unexpectedly.

Luke stared in astonishment. She was nodding her head and smiling rather sadly.

"A long time ago. He was such a promising boy. I had helped him, you know, to educate himself. And I was so proud of his—his spirit and the way he was determined to succeed."

She sighed again.

"My people, of course, were scandalised. Class distinctions in those days were very strong." She added after a minute or two, "I've always followed his career with great interest. My people, I think, were wrong."

Then, with a smile, she nodded a farewell and went back into the house.

Luke tried to collect his thoughts. He had placed Miss Waynflete as definitely "old." He realised now that she was probably still under sixty. Lord Whitfield must be well over fifty. She might, perhaps, be a year or two older than he, no more.

And he was going to marry Bridget. Bridget, who was twenty-eight. Bridget, who was young and alive. . . .

"Oh, damn," said Luke. "Don't let me go on thinking of it. The job. Get on with the job."

CHAPTER FOURTEEN

Meditations of Luke

MRS. CHURCH, Amy Gibbs's aunt, was definitely an unpleasant woman. Her sharp nose, shifty eyes, and her voluble tongue all alike filled Luke with nausea.

He adopted a curt manner with her and found it unexpectedly successful.

"What you've got to do," he told her, "is to answer my questions to the best of your ability. If you hold back anything or tamper with the truth the consequences may be extremely serious to you."

"Yes, sir. I see. I'm sure I'm only too willing to tell you anything I can. I've never been mixed up with the police——"

"And you don't want to be," finished Luke. "Well, if you do as I've told you there won't be any question of that. I want to know all about your late niece—who her friends were—what money she had—anything she said that might be out of the way. We'll start with her friends. Who were they?"

Mrs. Church leered at him slyly out of the corner of an unpleasant eye.

"You'll be meaning gentlemen, sir?"

"Had she any girl friends?"

"Well—hardly—not to speak of, sir. Of course there was girls she'd been in service with—but Amy didn't keep up with them much. You see——"

"She preferred the sterner sex. Go on. Tell me about that."

"It was Jim Harvey down at the garage she was actually going with, sir. And a nice steady young fellow he was. 'You couldn't do better,' I've said to her many a time——"

Luke cut in:

"And the others?"

Again he got the sly look.

"I expect you're thinking of the gentleman who keeps the curiosity shop? I didn't like it myself, and I tell you that straight, sir! I've always been respectable and I don't hold with carryings on! But with what girls are nowadays it's no use speaking to them. They go their own way. And often they live to regret it."

"Did Amy live to regret it?" asked Luke bluntly.

"No, sir—that I do *not* think."

"She went to consult Dr. Thomas on the day of her death. That wasn't the reason?"

"No, sir, I'm nearly sure it wasn't. Oh! I'd take my oath on it! Amy had been feeling ill and out of sorts, but it was just a bad cough and cold she had. It wasn't anything of the kind you suggest, I'm sure it wasn't, sir."

"I'll take your word for that. How far had matters gone between her and Ellsworthy?"

Mrs. Church leered.

"I couldn't exactly say, sir. Amy wasn't one for confiding in me."

Luke said curtly:

"But they'd gone pretty far?"

Mrs. Church said smoothly:

"The gentleman hasn't got at all a good reputation here, sir. All sorts of goings on. And friends down from town and many very queer happenings. Up in the Witches' Meadow in the middle of the night."

"Did Amy go?"

"She did go once, sir, I believe. Stayed out all night and his lordship found out about it (she was at the Manor then) and spoke to her pretty sharp, and she sauced him back and he gave her notice for it, which was only to be expected."

"Did she ever talk to you much about what went on in the places she was in?"

Mrs. Church shook her head.

"Not very much, sir. More interested in her own doings, she was."

"She was with Major and Mrs. Horton for a while, wasn't she?"

"Nearly a year, sir."

"Why did she leave?"

"Just to better herself. There was a place going at the Manor, and of course the wages was better there."

Luke nodded.

"She was with the Hortons at the time of Mrs. Horton's death?" he asked.

"Yes, sir. She grumbled a lot about that—with two hospital nurses in the house, and all the extra work nurses make, and the trays and one thing and another."

"She wasn't with Mr. Abbot, the lawyer, at all?"

"No, sir. Mr. Abbot has a man and wife do for him. Amy did go to see him once at his office, but I don't know why."

Luke stored away that small fact as possibly relevant. Since Mrs. Church, however, clearly knew nothing more about it, he did not pursue the subject.

"Any other gentlemen in the town who were friends of hers?"

" Nothing that I'd care to repeat."

" Come now, Mrs. Church. I want the truth, remember."

" It wasn't a gentleman, sir, very far from it. Demeaning herself, that's what it was, and so I told her."

" Do you mind speaking more plainly, Mrs. Church?"

" You'll have heard of the Seven Stars, sir? *Not* a good-class house, and the landlord, Harry Carter, a low-class fellow and half-seas over most of the time."

" Amy was a friend of his?"

" She went a walk with him once or twice. I don't believe there was more in it than that. I don't indeed, sir."

Luke nodded thoughtfully and changed the subject.

" Did you know a small boy, Tommy Pierce?"

" What? Mrs. Pierce's son? Of course I did. Always up to mischief."

" He ever see much of Amy?"

" Oh, no, sir. Amy would soon send him off with a flea in his ear if he tried any of his tricks on her."

" Was she happy in her place with Miss Waynflete?"

" She found it a bit dull, sir, and the pay wasn't high. But of course after she'd been dismissed the way she was from Ashe Manor, it wasn't so easy to get another good place."

" She could have gone away, I suppose?"

" To London, you mean?"

" Or some other part of the country?"

Mrs. Church shook her head. She said slowly:

" Amy didn't want to leave Wychwood—not as things were."

" How do you mean, *as things were*?"

" What with Jim and the gentleman at the curio shop."

Luke nodded thoughtfully. Mrs. Church went on:

" Miss Waynflete is a very nice lady, but very particular about brass and silver and everything being dusted and the mattresses turned. Amy wouldn't have put up with the fussing if she hadn't been enjoying herself in other ways."

" I can imagine that," said Luke dryly.

He turned things over in his mind. He could see no further questions to ask. He was fairly certain that he had extracted all that Mrs. Church knew. He decided on one last tentative attack.

" I dare say you can guess the reason of all these questions.

The circumstances of Amy's death were rather mysterious. We're not entirely satisfied as to its being an accident. If not, you realise what it must have been."

Mrs. Church said with a certain ghoulish relish:

" Foul play!"

" Quite so. Now supposing your niece *did* meet with foul play, who do you think is likely to be responsible for her death?"

Mrs. Church wiped her hands on her apron.

" There'd be a reward, as likely as not, for setting the police on the right track," she inquired meaningly.

" There might be," said Luke.

" I wouldn't like to say anything definite," Mrs. Church passed a hungry tongue over her thin lips. " But the gentleman at the curio shop is a queer one. You'll remember the Castor case, sir—and how they found little bits of the poor girl pinned up all over Castor's seaside bungalow and how they found five or six other poor girls he'd served the same way. Maybe this Mr. Ellsworthy is one of that kind?"

" That's your suggestion, is it?"

" Well, it might be that way, sir, mightn't it?"

Luke admitted that it might. Then he said:

" Was Ellsworthy away from here on the afternoon of Derby Day? That's a very important point."

Mrs. Church stared.

" Derby Day?"

" Yes—a fortnight ago last Wednesday."

She shook her head.

" Really, I couldn't say as to that. He usually was away on Wednesdays—went up to town as often as not. It's early closing Wednesday, you see."

" Oh," said Luke. " Early closing."

He took his leave of Mrs. Church, disregarding her insinuations that her time had been valuable and that she was therefore entitled to monetary compensation. He found himself disliking Mrs. Church intensely. Nevertheless the conversation he had had with her, though not strikingly illuminative in any way, had provided several suggestive small points.

He went over things carefully in his mind.

Yes, it still boiled down to those four people. Thomas,

Abbot, Horton and Ellsworthy. The attitude of Miss Wayn-flete seemed to him to prove that.

Her distress and reluctance to mention a name. Surely that meant, that *must* mean, that the person in question was some one of standing in Wychwood, some one whom a chance insinuation might definitely injure. It tallied, too, with Miss Pinkerton's determination to take her suspicions to head-quarters. The local police would ridicule her theory.

It was not a case of the butcher, the baker, the candlestick-maker. It was not a case of a mere garage mechanic. The person in question was one against whom an accusation of murder was a fantastic and, moreover, a serious matter.

There were four possible candidates. It was up to him to go carefully once more into the case against each one and make up his own mind.

First to examine the reluctance of Miss Waynflete. She was a conscientious and scrupulous person. She believed that she knew the man whom Miss Pinkerton had suspected, but it was, as she had pointed out, only a *belief* on her part. It was possible that she was mistaken.

Who was the person in Miss Waynflete's mind?

Miss Waynflete was distressed lest an accusation by her might injure an innocent man. Therefore the object of her sus-picions *must* be a man of high standing, generally liked and respected by the community.

Therefore, Luke argued, that automatically barred out Ells-worthy. He was practically a stranger to Wychwood, his local reputation was bad, not good. Luke did not believe that, if Ellsworthy was the person in Miss Waynflete's mind, she would have had any objection to mentioning him. Therefore as far as Miss Waynflete was concerned, wash out Ellsworthy.

Now as to the others. Luke believed that he could also elim-inate Major Horton. Miss Waynflete had rebutted with some warmth the suggestion that Horton might have poisoned his wife. If she had suspected him of later crimes, she would hardly have been so positive about his innocence of the death of Mrs. Horton.

That left Dr. Thomas and Mr. Abbot. Both of them fulfilled the necessary requirements. They were men of high profes-sional standing against whom no word of scandal had ever been uttered. They were, on the whole, both popular and well liked, and were known as men of integrity and rectitude.

Luke proceeded to another aspect of the matter. Could he, himself, eliminate Ellsworthy and Horton? Immediately he shook his head. It was not so simple. Miss Pinkerton had *known*—really known—who the man was. That was proved, in the first case by her own death, and in the second case, by the death of Dr. Humbleby. But Miss Pinkerton had never actually mentioned a *name* to Honoria Waynflete. Therefore, though Miss Waynflete *thought* she knew, she might quite easily be wrong. We often *know* what other people are thinking—but sometimes we find out that we did not know after all—and have, in fact, made an egregious mistake!

Therefore the four candidates were still in the field. Miss Pinkerton was dead and could give no further assistance. It was up to Luke to do what he had done before, on the day after he came to Wychwood, weigh up the evidence and consider the probabilities.

He began with Ellsworthy. On the face of it Ellsworthy was the likeliest starter. He was abnormal and had possibly a perverted personality. He might quite easily be a " lust killer."

" Let's take it this way," said Luke to himself. " Suspect every one in turn. Ellsworthy, for instance. Let's say he's the killer! For the moment, let's take it quite definitely that I know that. Now we'll take the possible victims in chronological order. First, Mrs. Horton. Difficult to see what motive Ellsworthy could have had for doing away with Mrs. Horton. But there was a *means*. Horton spoke of some quack nostrum that she got from him and took. Some poison like arsenic could have been given that way. The question is —Why?

" Now the others. Amy Gibbs. Why did Ellsworthy kill Amy Gibbs? The obvious reason—she was being a nuisance! Threatened an action for breach of promise, perhaps? Or had she assisted at a midnight orgy? Did she threaten to talk? Lord Whitfield has a good deal of influence in Wychwood and Lord Whitfield, according to Bridget, is a very moral man. He might have taken up the matter against Ellsworthy if the latter had been up to anything particularly obscene. So—exit

Amy. Not, I think, a sadistic murder. The method employed is against that.

" Who's next—Carter? Why Carter? Unlikely *he* would know about midnight orgies (or did Amy tell him?). Was the pretty daughter mixed up in it? Did Ellsworthy start making love to her? (Must have a look at Lucy Carter.) Perhaps he was just abusive to Ellsworthy, and Ellsworthy in his cat-like feline way, resented it. If he'd already committed one or two murders he would be getting sufficiently callous to contemplate a killing for a very slight reason.

" Now Tommy Pierce. Why did Ellsworthy kill Tommy Pierce? Easy. Tommy had assisted at a midnight ritual of some kind. Tommy threatened to talk about it. Perhaps Tommy *was* talking about it. Shut Tommy's mouth.

" Dr. Humbleby. Why did Ellsworthy kill Dr. Humbleby? That's the easiest of the lot! Humbleby was a doctor and he'd noticed that Ellsworthy's mental balance was none too good. Probably was getting ready to do something about it. So Humbleby was doomed. There's a stumbling block there in the method. How did Ellsworthy ensure that Humbleby should die of blood poisoning? Or did Humbleby die of something else? Was the poisoned finger a coincidence?

" Last of all, Miss Pinkerton. Wednesday's early closing. Ellsworthy might have gone up to town that day. Has he a car, I wonder? Never seen him in one, but that proves nothing. He knew she'd suspected him and he was going to take no chances of Scotland Yard believing her story. Perhaps they already knew something about him then?

" That's the case against Ellsworthy! Now what is there *for* him? Well, for one thing, he's certainly not the man Miss Waynflete *thought* Miss Pinkerton meant. For another, he doesn't fit—quite—with my own vague impression. When she was talking I got a picture of a man—and it wasn't a man like Ellsworthy. The impression she gave me was of a very normal man—outwardly, that is—the kind of man nobody would suspect. Ellsworthy is the kind of man you *would* suspect. No, I got more the impression of a man like—Dr. Thomas.

" Thomas, now. What about Thomas? I wiped him clean off the list after I'd had a chat with him. Nice unassuming fellow. But the whole point of this murderer—unless I've got the whole thing wrong—is that he would be a nice unassuming fellow. The last person you'd think ever would be a murderer! Which, of course, is exactly what one feels about Thomas.

"Now then, let's go through it all again. Why did Dr. Thomas kill Amy Gibbs? Really, it seems most unlikely that he did! But she *did* go to see him that day, and he *did* give her that bottle of cough mixture. Suppose that was really oxalic acid. That would be very simple and clever! Who was called in, I wonder, when she was found poisoned—Humbleby or Thomas? If it was Thomas he might just come along with an old bottle of hat paint in his pocket, put it down unobtrusively on the table—and take off both bottles to be analysed as bold as brass! Something like that. It could be done if you were cool enough!

"Tommy Pierce? Again I can't see a likely motive. That's the difficulty with our Dr. Thomas—*motive*. There's not even a crazy motive! Same with Carter. Why should Dr. Thomas want to dispose of Carter? One can only assume that Amy, Tommy and the publican all knew something about Dr. Thomas that it was unhealthy to know. Ah! Supposing now that that something was *the death of Mrs. Horton.* Dr. Thomas attended her. And she died of a rather unexpected relapse. He could have managed that easily enough. And Amy Gibbs, remember, was in the house at the time. She might have seen or heard something. That would account for *her.* Tommy Pierce, we have it on good authority, was a particularly inquisitive small boy. He *may* have got wise to something. Can't get Carter in. Amy Gibbs told him something. He may have repeated it in his cups, and Thomas may have decided to silence him too. All this, of course, is pure conjecture. But what else can one do?

"Now Humbleby. Ah! At last we come to a perfectly plausible murder. Adequate motive and ideal means! If Dr. Thomas couldn't give his partner blood poisoning, no one could! He could reinfect the wound every time he dressed it! I wish the earlier killings were a little more plausible.

"Miss Pinkerton? She's more difficult, but there is one

definite fact. Dr. Thomas was not in Wychwood for at least a good part of the day. He gave out that he was attending a confinement. That may be. But the fact remains that he was away from Wychwood *in a car*.

"Is there anything else? Yes, just one thing. The look he gave me when I went away from the house the other day. Superior, condescending, the smile of a man who'd just led me up the garden path and knew it."

Luke sighed, shook his head and went on with his reasoning.

"Abbot? He's the right kind of man too. Normal, well-to-do, respected, last sort of man, etc., etc. He's conceited, too, and confident. Murderers usually are! They've got over-weening conceit! Always think they'll get away with it. Amy Gibbs paid him a visit once. Why? What did she want to see him for? To get legal advice? Why? Or was it a personal matter? There's that mention of 'a letter from a lady' that Tommy saw. Was that letter from Amy Gibbs? Or was it a letter written by Mrs. Horton—a letter, perhaps, that Amy Gibbs had got hold of? What other lady could there be writing to Mr. Abbot on a matter so private that he loses control when the office boy inadvertently sees it? What else can we think of re Amy Gibbs? The hat paint? Yes, right kind of old-fashioned touch—men like Abbot are usually well behind the times where women are concerned. The old-world style of philanderer! Tommy Pierce? Obvious—on account of the letter (really, it must have been a very damning letter!). Carter? Well, there was trouble about Carter's daughter. Abbot wasn't going to have a scandal—a low-down ruffianly halfwit like Carter dare to threaten him! He who had got away with two clever killings! Away with Mr. Carter! Dark night and a well-directed push. Really, this killing business is almost too easy.

"Have I got the Abbot mentality? I think so. Nasty look in an old lady's eye. She's thinking things about him. . . . Then, row with Humbleby. Old Humbleby daring to set himself against Abbot, the clever solicitor and murderer. The old fool—he little knows what's in store for him! *He's* for it! Daring to browbeat me!

"And then—what? Turning to catch Lavinia Pinkerton's eyes. And his own eyes falter—show a consciousness of guilt.

He who was boasting of being unsuspected has definitely aroused suspicion. Miss Pinkerton knows his secret. . . . She knows what he has done. . . . Yes, but she can't have *proof*. But suppose she goes about looking for it. . . . Suppose she talks. . . . Suppose . . . He's quite a shrewd judge of character. He guesses what she will finally do. If she goes with this tale of hers to Scotland Yard they *may* believe her —they *may* start making inquiries. Something pretty desperate has got to be done. Has Abbot got a car or did he hire one in London? Anyway, he was away from here on Derby Day. . . ."

Again Luke paused. He was so entering into the spirit of the thing that he found it hard to make a transition from one suspect to another. He had to wait a minute before he could force himself into the mood where he could visualise Major Horton as a successful murderer.

"Horton murdered his wife. Let's start with that! He had ample provocation and he gained considerably by her death. In order to carry it off successfully he had to make a good show of devotion. He's had to keep that up. Sometimes, shall we say, he overdoes it a bit?

"Very good, one murder successfully accomplished. Who's the next? Amy Gibbs. Yes, perfectly credible. Amy was in the house. She may have seen something—the major administering a soothing cup of beef-tea or gruel? She mayn't have realised the point of what she saw till some time later. The hat paint trick is the sort of thing that would occur to the major quite naturally—a very masculine man with little knowledge of women's fripperies.

"Amy Gibbs all serene and accounted for.

"The drunken Carter? Same suggestion as before. Amy told him something. Another straightforward murder.

"Now Tommy Pierce. We've got to fall back on his inquisitive nature. I suppose the letter in Abbot's office couldn't have been a complaint from Mrs. Horton that her husband was trying to poison her? That's a wild suggestion, but it *might* be so. Anyway, the major becomes alive to the fact that Tommy is a menace, so Tommy joins Amy and Carter. All quite simple and straightforward and according to Cocker. Easy to kill? My God, yes.

"But now we come to something rather more difficult. Humbleby! Motive? Very obscure. Humbleby was attending Mrs. Horton originally. Did he get puzzled by the illness, and did Horton influence his wife to change to the younger, more unsuspicious doctor? But if so, *what made Humbleby a danger so long after?* Difficult, that. . . . The manner of his death, too. A poisoned finger. Doesn't connect up with the major.

"Miss Pinkerton? That's perfectly possible. He has a car. I saw it. And he was away from Wychwood that day, supposedly gone to the Derby. It might be—yes. *Is* Horton a cold-blooded killer? Is he? Is he? I wish I knew. . . ."

Luke stared ahead of him. His brow was puckered with thought.

"It's one of them. . . . I don't *think* it's Ellsworthy—but it might be! He's the most obvious one! Thomas is wildly unlikely—if it weren't for the *manner* of Humbleby's death. That blood poisoning definitely points to a *medical* murderer! It *could* be Abbot—there's not as much evidence against him as against the others—but I can *see* him in the part, somehow. . . . Yes—he fits as the others don't. And it *could* be Horton! Bullied by his wife for years, feeling his insignificance—yes, it could be! But Miss Waynflete doesn't think it is, and she's no fool—and she knows the place and the people in it. . . .

"Which *does* she suspect, Abbot or Thomas? It must be one of these two. . . . If I tackled her outright—'Which of them is it? '—I'd get it out of her then, perhaps.

"But even then she might be wrong. There's no way of proving *her* right—like Miss Pinkerton proved herself. More evidence—that's what I want. If there were to be one more case—just one more—then I'd know——"

He stopped himself with a start.

"My God," he said under his breath. "What I'm asking for is *another murder*. . . ."

CHAPTER FIFTEEN

Improper Conduct of a Chauffeur

IN THE bar of the Seven Stars Luke drank his pint and felt somewhat embarrassed. The stare of half a dozen bucolic pairs of eyes followed his least movement, and conversation had come to a standstill upon his entrance. Luke essayed a few comments of general interest such as the crops, the state of the weather, and football coupons, but to none did he get any response.

He was reduced to gallantry. The fine-looking girl behind the counter with her black hair and red cheeks he rightly judged to be Miss Lucy Carter.

His advances were received in a pleasant spirit. Miss Carter duly giggled and said, " Go on with you! I'm sure you don't think nothing of the kind! That's telling!"—and other such rejoinders. But the performance was clearly mechanical.

Luke, seeing no advantage to be gained by remaining, finished his beer and departed. He walked along the path to where the river was spanned by a footbridge. He was standing looking at this when a quavering voice behind him said:

" That's it, mister, that's where old Harry went over."

Luke turned to see one of his late fellow-drinkers, one who had been particularly unresponsive to the topic of crops, weather and coupons. He was now clearly about to enjoy himself as a guide to the macabre.

" Went over into the mud, he did," said the ancient labourer. " Right into the mud and stuck in it head downwards."

" Odd he should have fallen off here," said Luke.

" He were drunk, he were," said the rustic indulgently.

" Yes, but he must have come this way drunk many times before."

" Most every night," said the other. " Always in liquor, Harry were."

" Perhaps some one pushed him over," said Luke, making the suggestion in a casual fashion.

124

"They might of," the rustic agreed. "But I don't know who'd go for to do that," he added.

"He might have made a few enemies. He was fairly abusive when he was drunk, wasn't he?"

"His language was a treat to hear! Didn't mince his words, Harry didn't. But no one would go for to push a man what's drunk."

Luke did not combat this statement. It was evidently regarded as wildly unsporting for advantage to be taken of a man's state of intoxication. The rustic had sounded quite shocked at the idea.

"Well," he said vaguely, "it was a sad business."

"None so sad for his missus," said the old man. "Reckon her and Lucy haven't no call to be sad about it."

"There may be other people who are glad to have him out of the way."

The old man was vague about that.

"Maybe," he said. "But he didn't mean no harm, Harry didn't."

On this epitaph for the late Mr. Carter, they parted.

Luke bent his steps towards the old Hall. The library transacted its business in the two front rooms. Luke passed on to the back through a door which was labelled Museum. There he moved from case to case, studying the not very inspiring exhibits. Some Roman pottery and coins. Some South Sea curiosities, a Malay head-dress. Various Indian gods "presented by Major Horton," together with a large and malevolent-looking Buddha, and a case of doubtful-looking Egyptian beads.

Luke wandered out again into the hall. There was no one about. He went quietly up the stairs. There was a room with magazines and papers there, and a room filled with nonfiction books.

Luke went a story higher. Here were rooms filled with what he designated to himself as junk. Stuffed birds removed from the museum owing to the moth having attacked them, stacks of torn magazines and a room whose shelves were covered with out-of-date works of fiction and children's books.

Luke approached the window. Here it must have been that Tommy Pierce had sat, possibly whistling and occasionally rubbing a pane of glass vigorously when he heard any one coming.

Somebody had come in. Tommy had shown his zeal—sitting half out of the window and polishing with zest. And then that somebody had come up to him, and while talking, had given a sudden sharp push.

Luke turned away. He walked down the stairs and stood a minute or two in the hall. Nobody had noticed him come in. Nobody had seen him go upstairs.

"*Any one* might have done it!" said Luke. "Easiest thing in the world."

He heard footsteps coming from the direction of the library proper. Since he was an innocent man with no objection to being seen, he could remain where he was. If he had not wanted to be seen, how easy just to step back inside the door of the museum room!

Miss Waynflete came out from the library, a little pile of books under her arm. She was pulling on her gloves. She looked happy and busy. When she saw him her face lit up and she exclaimed:

"Oh, Mr. Fitzwilliam, have you been looking at the museum? I'm afraid there isn't very much there, really. Lord Whitfield is talking of getting us some really interesting exhibits."

"Really?"

"Yes, something modern, you know, and up to date. Like they have at the Science Museum in London. He suggests a model aeroplane and a locomotive and some chemical things too."

"That would, perhaps, brighten things up."

"Yes, I don't think a museum should deal solely with the past, do you?"

"Perhaps not."

"Then some food exhibits, too—calories and vitamins—all that sort of thing. Lord Whitfield is so keen on the Greater Fitness Campaign."

"So he was saying the other night."

"It's *the* thing at present, isn't it? Lord Whitfield was telling me how he'd been to the Wellerman Institute—and seen such a lot of germs and cultures and bacteria—it quite made me shiver. And he told me all about mosquitoes and sleeping sickness and something about a liver fluke that I'm afraid was a little too difficult for *me*."

"It was probably too difficult for Lord Whitfield," said Luke cheerfully. "I'll bet he got it all wrong! You've got a much clearer brain than he has, Miss Waynflete."

Miss Waynflete said sedately:

"That's very nice of you, Mr. Fitzwilliam, but I'm afraid women are never quite such deep thinkers as men."

Luke repressed a desire to criticise adversely Lord Whitfield's processes of thought. Instead he said:

"I did look into the museum but afterwards I went up to have a look at the top windows."

"You mean where Tommy——" Miss Waynflete shivered. "It's really very horrible."

"Yes, it's not a nice thought. I've spent about an hour with Mrs. Church—Amy's aunt—not a nice woman!"

"Not at all."

"I had to take rather a strong line with her," said Luke. "I fancy she thinks I'm a kind of super policeman."

He stopped as he noted a sudden change of expression on Miss Waynflete's face.

"Oh, Mr. Fitzwilliam, do you think that was wise?"

Luke said:

"I don't really know. I think it was inevitable. The book story was wearing thin—I can't get much further on that. I had to ask the kind of questions that were directly to the point."

Miss Waynflete shook her head—the troubled expression still on her face.

"In a place like this, you see—everything gets round so fast."

"You mean that everybody will say 'there goes the tec' as I walk down the street? I don't think that really matters now. In fact, I may get more that way."

"I wasn't thinking of that." Miss Waynflete sounded a little breathless. "What I meant was—that *he*'ll know. *He*'ll realise that you're on his track."

Luke said slowly:

"I suppose he will."

Miss Waynflete said:

"But don't you see—that's horribly dangerous. *Horribly!*"

"You mean——" Luke grasped her point at last, "you mean that the killer will have a crack at *me?*"

"Yes."

"Funny," said Luke. "I never thought of that! I believe you're right, though. Well, that might be the best thing that could happen."

Miss Waynflete said earnestly:

"I don't think you realise that he's—he's a very clever man. He's cautious, too! And remember, he's got a great deal of experience—perhaps more than *we* know."

"Yes," said Luke thoughtfully. "That's probably true."

Miss Waynflete exclaimed:

"Oh, I don't like it! Really, I feel quite *alarmed*!"

Luke said gently:

"You needn't worry. I shall be very much on my guard I can assure you. You see I've narrowed the possibilities down pretty closely. I've an idea at any rate who the killer might be. . . ."

She looked up sharply.

Luke came a step nearer. He lowered his voice to a whisper:

"Miss Waynflete, if I were to ask you *which of two* men you considered the most likely—Dr. Thomas or Mr. Abbot—*what would you say?*"

"Oh——" said Miss Waynflete. Her hand flew to her breast. She stepped back. Her eyes met Luke's in an expression that puzzled him. They showed impatience and something closely allied to it that he could not quite place.

She said:

"I can't say anything——"

She turned away abruptly with a curious sound—half a sigh, half a sob.

Luke resigned himself.

"Are you going home?" he asked.

"No, I was going to take these books to Mrs. Humbleby. That lies on your way back to the Manor. We might go part of the way together."

"That will be very nice," said Luke.

They went down the steps, turned to the left skirting the village green.

Luke looked back at the stately lines of the house they had left.

" It must have been a lovely house in your father's day," he said.

Miss Waynflete sighed.

" Yes, we were all very happy there. I am so thankful it hasn't been pulled down. So many of the old houses are going."

" I know. It's sad."

" And really the new ones aren't nearly as well built."

" I doubt if they will stand the test of time as well."

" But of course," said Miss Waynflete, " the new ones *are* convenient—so labour saving, and not such big draughty passages to scrub."

Luke assented.

When they arrived at the gate of Dr. Humbleby's house, Miss Waynflete hesitated and said:

" Such a beautiful evening. I think, if you don't mind, I will come a little farther. I am enjoying the air."

Somewhat surprised, Luke expressed pleasure politely. It was hardly what he would have described as a beautiful evening. There was a strong wind blowing, turning back the leaves viciously on the trees. A storm, he thought, might come at any minute.

Miss Waynflete, however, clutching her hat with one hand, walked by his side with every appearance of enjoyment, talking as she went in little gasps.

It was a somewhat lonely lane they were taking, since from Dr. Humbleby's house the shortest way to Ashe Manor was not by the main road, but by a side lane which led to one of the back gates of the Manor House. This gate was not of the same ornate ironwork but had two handsome gate pillars surmounted by two vast pink pine-apples. Why pine-apples, Luke had been unable to discover! But he gathered that to Lord Whitfield pine-apples spelt distinction and good taste.

As they approached the gate the sound of voices raised in anger came to them. A moment later they came in sight of Lord Whitfield confronting a young man in chauffeur's uniform.

" You're fired," Lord Whitfield was shouting. " D'you hear? You're fired."

" If you'd overlook it, m'lord—just this once."

" No, I won't overlook it! Taking my car out. *My* car —and what's more you've been drinking—yes, you have, don't deny it! I've made it clear there are three things I won't have on my estate—one's drunkenness, another's immorality and the other's impertinence."

Though the man was not actually drunk, he had had enough to loosen his tongue. His manner changed.

" You won't have this and you won't have that, you old bastard! *Your* estate! Think we don't all know your father kept a boot-shop down here? Makes us laugh ourselves sick, it does, seeing you strutting about as cock of the walk! Who are you, I'd like to know? You're no better than I am— that's what you are."

Lord Whitfield turned purple.

" How dare you speak to me like that? How dare you?"

The young man took a threatening step forward.

" If you wasn't such a miserable pot-bellied little swine I'd give you a sock on the jaw—yes, I would."

Lord Whitfield hastily retreated a step, tripped over a root and went down in a sitting position.

Luke had come up.

" Get out of here," he said roughly to the chauffeur.

The latter regained sanity. He looked frightened.

" I'm sorry, sir. I don't know what came over me, I'm sure."

" A couple of glasses too much, I should say," said Luke.

He assisted Lord Whitfield to his feet.

" I—I beg your pardon, m'lord," stammered the man.

" You'll be sorry for this, Rivers," said Lord Whitfield.

His voice trembled with intense feeling.

The man hesitated a minute, then shambled away slowly.

Lord Whitfield exploded:

" Colossal impertinence! To me. Speaking to me like that. Something very serious will happen to that man! No respect —no proper sense of his station in life. When I think of what I do for these people—good wages—every comfort—a pension when they retire. The ingratitude—the base ingratitude . . ."

He choked with excitement, then perceived Miss Waynflete who was standing silently by.

" Is that you, Honoria? I'm deeply distressed you should have witnessed such a disgraceful scene. That man's language——"

" I'm afraid he wasn't quite himself, Lord Whitfield," said Miss Waynflete primly.

" He was drunk, that's what he was, drunk! "

" Just a bit lit up," said Luke.

" Do you know what he did?" Lord Whitfield looked from one to the other of them. " Took out my car—*my* car! Thought I shouldn't be back so soon. Bridget drove me over to Lyne in the two-seater. And this fellow had the impertinence to take a girl—Lucy Carter, I believe,—out in *my* car!"

Miss Waynflete said gently:

" A most improper thing to do."

Lord Whitfield seemed a little comforted.

" Yes, wasn't it?"

" But I'm sure he'll regret it."

" I shall see that he does!"

" You've dismissed him," Miss Waynflete pointed out.

Lord Whitfield shook his head.

" He'll come to a bad end, that fellow."

He threw back his shoulders.

" Come up to the house, Honoria, and have a glass of sherry."

" Thank you, Lord Whitfield, but I must go to Mrs. Humbleby with these books. Good-night, Mr. Fitzwilliam. You'll be *quite* all right now."

She gave him a smiling nod and walked briskly away. It was so much the attitude of a nurse who delivers a child at a party that Luke caught his breath as a sudden idea struck him. Was it possible that Miss Waynflete had accompanied him solely in order to protect him? The idea seemed ludicrous, but——

Lord Whitfield's voice interrupted his meditations.

" Very capable woman, Honoria Waynflete."

" Very, I should think."

Lord Whitfield began to walk towards the house. He moved rather stiffly and his hand went to his posterior and rubbed it gingerly.

Suddenly he chuckled.

" I was engaged to Honoria once—years ago. She was a nice-looking girl—not so skinny as she is to-day. Seems funny to think of now. Her people were the nobs of this place."

" Yes?"

Lord Whitfield ruminated :

" Old Colonel Waynflete bossed the show. One had to come out and touch one's cap pretty sharp. One of the old school he was, and proud as Lucifer."

He chuckled again.

" The fat was in the fire all right when Honoria announced she was going to marry me! Called herself a Radical, she did. Very earnest. Was all for abolishing class distinctions. She was a serious kind of girl."

" So her family broke up the romance?"

Lord Whitfield rubbed his nose.

" Well—not exactly. Matter of fact we had a bit of a row over something. Blinking bird she had—one of those beastly twittering canaries—always hated them—bad business —wrung its neck. Well—no good dwelling on all that now. Let's forget it."

He shook his shoulders like a man who throws off an un-pleasant memory.

Then he said, rather jerkily :

" Don't think she's ever forgiven me. Well, perhaps it's only natural. . . ."

" I think she's forgiven you all right," said Luke.

Lord Whitfield brightened up.

" Do you? Glad of that. You know I respect Honoria. Capable woman *and* a lady! That still counts even in these days. She runs that library business very well."

He looked up and his voice changed.

" Hallo," he said. " Here comes Bridget."

CHAPTER SIXTEEN

The Pine-apple

LUKE FELT a tightening of his muscles as Bridget approached.

He had had no word alone with her since the day of the tennis party. By mutual consent they had avoided each other. He stole a glance at her now.

She looked provokingly calm, cool and indifferent.

She said lightly:

"I was beginning to wonder what on earth had become of you, Gordon?"

Lord Whitfield grunted:

"Had a bit of a dust up! That fellow Rivers had the impertinence to take the Rolls out this afternoon."

"*Lèse-majesté*," said Bridget.

"It's no good making a joke out of it, Bridget. The thing's serious. He took a girl out."

"I don't suppose it would have given him any pleasure to go solemnly for a drive by himself!"

Lord Whitfield drew himself up.

"On my estate I'll have decent moral behaviour."

"It isn't actually immoral to take a girl joy riding."

"It is when it's *my* car."

"That, of course, is worse than immorality! It practically amounts to blasphemy. But you can't cut out the sex stuff altogether, Gordon. The moon is at the full and it's actually Midsummer Eve."

"Is it, by Jove?" said Luke.

Bridget threw him a glance.

"That seems to interest you?"

"It does."

Bridget turned back to Lord Whitfield.

"Three extraordinary people have arrived at the Bells and Motley. Item one, a man with shorts, spectacles and a lovely plum-coloured silk shirt! Item two, a female with no eyebrows, dressed in a peplum, a pound of assorted sham Egyptian beads and sandals. Item three, a fat man in a lavender suit and co-respondent shoes. I suspect them of being friends of our Mr. Ellsworthy! Says the gossip writer: ' Some one has whispered that there will be gay doings in the Witches' Meadow to-night.' "

Lord Whitfield turned purple and said:

" I won't have it! "

" You can't help it, darling. The Witches' Meadow is public property."

" I won't have this irreligious mumbo jumbo going on down here! I'll expose it in *Scandals.*" He paused, then said, " Remind me to make a note about that and get Siddely on to it. I must go up to town to-morrow."

" Lord Whitfield's campaign against witchcraft," said Bridget flippantly. " Medieval superstitions still rife in quiet country village."

Lord Whitfield stared at her with a puzzled frown, then he turned and went into the house.

Luke said pleasantly:

" You must do your stuff better than that, Bridget! "

" What do you mean?"

" It would be a pity if you lost your job! That hundred thousand isn't yours yet. Nor are the diamonds and pearls. I should wait until after the marriage ceremony to exercise your sarcastic gifts if I were you."

Her glance met his coolly.

" You are so thoughtful, dear Luke. It's kind of you to take my future so much to heart! "

" Kindness and consideration have always been my strong points."

" I hadn't noticed it."

" No? You surprise me."

Bridget twitched the leaf off a creeper. She said:

" What have you been doing to-day?"

" The usual spot of sleuthing."

" Any results?"

" Yes and no, as the politicians say. By the way, have you got any tools in the house?"

" I expect so. What kind of tools?"

"Oh, any handy little gadgets. Perhaps I could inspect same."

Ten minutes later Luke had made his selection from a cupboard shelf.

"That little lot will do nicely," he said slapping the pocket in which he had stowed them away.

"Are you thinking of doing a spot of forcing and entering?"

"Maybe."

"You're very uncommunicative on the subject."

"Well, after all, the situation bristles with difficulties. I'm in the hell of a position. After our little knock up on Saturday I suppose I ought to clear out of here."

"To behave as a perfect gentleman, you should."

"But since I'm convinced that I am pretty hot on the trail of a homicidal maniac, I'm more or less forced to remain. If you could think of any convincing reason for me to leave here and take up my quarters at the Bells and Motley, for goodness sake trot it out."

Bridget shook her head.

"That's not feasible—you being a cousin and all that. Besides the inn is full of Mr. Ellsworthy's friends. They only run to three guest rooms."

"So I am forced to remain, painful as it must be for you."

Bridget smiled sweetly at him.

"Not at all. I can always do with a few scalps to dangle."

"That," said Luke appreciatively, "was a particularly dirty crack. What I admire about you, Bridget, is that you have practically no instincts of kindness. Well, well. The rejected lover will now go and change for dinner."

The evening passed uneventfully. Luke won Lord Whitfield's approval even more deeply than before by the apparent absorbed interest with which he listened to the other's nightly discourse.

When they came into the drawing-room Bridget said:

"You men have been a long time."

Luke replied:

"Lord Whitfield was being so interesting that the time passed like a flash. He was telling me how he founded his first newspaper."

Mrs. Anstruther said:

" These new little fruiting trees in pots are perfectly marvellous, I believe. You ought to try them along the terrace, Gordon."

The conversation then proceeded on normal lines.

Luke retired early.

He did not, however, go to bed. He had other plans.

It was just striking twelve when he descended the stairs noiselessly in tennis shoes, passed through the library and let himself out by a window.

The wind was still blowing in violent gusts interspersed with brief lulls. Clouds scudded across the sky, obliterating the moon so that darkness alternated with bright moonlight.

Luke made his way by a circuitous route to Mr. Ellsworthy's establishment. He saw his way clear to doing a little investigation. He was fairly certain that Ellsworthy and his friends would be out together on this particular date. Midsummer Eve, Luke thought, was sure to be marked by some ceremony or other. Whilst this was in progress, it would be a good opportunity to search Mr. Ellsworthy's house.

He climbed a couple of walls, got round to the back of the house, took the assorted tools from his pocket and selected a likely implement. He found a scullery window amenable to his efforts. A few minutes later he had slipped back the catch, raised the sash and hoisted himself over.

He had a torch in his pocket. He used it sparingly—a brief flash to show him his way and to avoid running into things.

In a quarter of an hour he had satisfied himself that the house was empty. The owner was out and abroad on his own affairs.

Luke smiled with satisfaction and settled down to his task.

He made a minute and thorough search of every available nook and corner. In a locked drawer, below two or three innocuous water-colour sketches, he came upon some artistic efforts which caused him to lift his eyebrows and whistle. Mr. Ellsworthy's correspondence was unilluminating, but some of his books—those tucked away at the back of a cupboard—repaid attention.

Besides these, Luke accumulated three meagre but suggestive

scraps of information. The first was a pencil scrawl in a little notebook. *"Settle with Tommy Pierce"*—the date being a couple of days before the boy's death. The second was a crayon sketch of Amy Gibbs with a furious red cross right across the face. The third was a bottle of cough mixture. None of these things were in any way conclusive, but taken together they might be considered as encouraging.

Luke was just restoring some final order, replacing things in their place, when he suddenly stiffened and switched off his torch.

He had heard the key inserted in the lock of a side door.

He stepped across to the door of the room he was in, and applied an eye to a crack. He hoped Ellsworthy, if it was he, would go straight upstairs.

The side door opened and Ellsworthy stepped in, switching on a hall light as he did so.

As he passed along the hall, Luke saw his face and caught his breath.

It was unrecognisable. There was foam on the lips, the eyes were alight with a strange mad exultation as he pranced along the hall in little dancing steps.

But what caused Luke to catch his breath was the sight of Ellsworthy's hands. They were stained a deep brownish red—the colour of dried blood. . . .

He disappeared up the stairs. A moment later the light in the hall was extinguished.

Luke waited a little longer, then very cautiously he crept out of the hall, made his way to the scullery and left by the window. He looked up at the house, but it was dark and silent.

He drew a deep breath.

" My God," he said, " the fellow's mad all right! I wonder what he's up to? I'll swear that was blood on his hands!"

He made a detour round the village and returned to Ashe Manor by a roundabout route. It was as he was turning into the side lane that a sudden rustle of leaves made him swing round.

" Who's there?"

A tall figure wrapped in a dark cloak came out from the

shadow of a tree. It looked so eerie that Luke felt his heart miss a beat. Then he recognised the long pale face under the hood.

" Bridget? How you startled me ! "

She said sharply :

" Where have you been? I saw you go out."

" And you followed me? "

" No. You'd gone too far. I've been waiting till you came back."

" That was a damned silly thing to do," Luke grumbled.

She repeated her question impatiently.

" Where have you been? "

Luke said gaily :

" Raiding our Mr. Ellsworthy ! "

Bridget caught her breath.

" Did you—find anything? "

" I don't know. I know a bit more about the swine—his pornographical tastes and all that, and there are three things that might be suggestive."

She listened attentively as he recounted the result of his search.

" It's very slight evidence, though," he ended. " But, Bridget, just as I was leaving Ellsworthy came back. And I tell you this—the man's as mad as a hatter ! "

" You really think so? "

" I saw his face—it was—unspeakable ! God knows what he'd been up to ! He was in a delirium of mad excitement. And his hands were stained. I'll swear with *blood*."

Bridget shivered.

" Horrible . . . " she murmured.

Luke said irritably :

" You shouldn't have come out by yourself, Bridget. It was absolute madness. Somebody might have knocked you on the head."

She laughed shakily.

" The same applies to you, my dear."

" I can look after myself."

" I'm pretty good at taking care of myself, too. Hard boiled, I should think you'd call me."

A sharp gust of wind came. Luke said suddenly :

" Take off that hood thing."

" Why?"

With an unexpected movement he snatched at her cloak and whipped it away. The wind caught her hair and blew it out straight up from her head. She stared at him, her breath coming fast.

Luke said:

" You certainly are incomplete without a broomstick, Bridget. That's how I saw you first." He stared a minute longer and said, " You're a cruel devil."

With a sharp impatient sigh he tossed the cloak back to her.

" There—put it on. Let's get home."

" Wait . . ."

" Why?"

She came up to him. She spoke in a low, rather breathless voice.

" Because I've got something to say to you—that's partly why I waited for you here—outside the Manor. I want to say it to you now—before we go inside—into Gordon's property . . ."

" Well?"

She gave a short, rather bitter laugh.

" Oh, it's quite simple. *You win*, Luke. That's all!"

He said sharply:

" What do you mean?"

" I mean that I've given up the idea of being Lady Whitfield."

He took a step nearer.

" Is that true?" he demanded.

" Yes, Luke."

" You'll marry me?"

" Yes."

" Why, I wonder?"

" I don't know. You say such beastly things to me—and I seem to like it. . . ."

He took her in his arms and kissed her. He said:

" It's a mad world!"

" Are you happy, Luke?"

" Not particularly."

" Do you think you'll ever be happy with me?"

" I don't know. I'll risk it."

" Yes—that's what I feel. . . ."

He slipped his arm through hers.

" We're rather queer about all this, my sweet. Come along. Perhaps we shall be more normal in the morning."

" Yes—it's rather frightening the way things happen to one. . . ." She looked down and tugged him to a standstill. " Luke—Luke—*what's that* . . .?"

The moon had come out from the clouds. Luke looked down to where Bridget's shoe trembled by a huddled mass.

With a startled exclamation he dragged his arm free and knelt down. He looked from the shapeless heap to the gate-post above. The pine-apple was gone.

He stood up at last. Bridget was standing, her hands pressed together on her mouth.

He said:

" It's the chauffeur—Rivers. He's dead . . ."

" That beastly stone thing—it's been loose for some time —I suppose it blew down on him?"

Luke shook his head.

" The wind wouldn't do a thing like that. Oh! that's what it's *meant* to look like—that's what it's *meant* to be—another accident! But it's a fake. *It's the killer again. . . .*"

" No—no, Luke——"

" I tell you it is. Do you know what I felt on the back of his head—in with the stickiness and mess—*grains of sand*. There's no sand about here. I tell you, Bridget, somebody stood here and slugged him as he came through the gate back to his cottage. Then laid him down and rolled that pine-apple thing down on top of him."

Bridget said faintly:

" Luke—there's blood—on your hands. . . ."

Luke said grimly:

" There was blood on someone else's hands. Do you know what I was thinking this afternoon—that if there were to be one more crime we'd surely know. And we *do* know! *Ells-worthy!* He was out to-night and he came in with blood on his hands capering and prancing and mad—drunk with the homicidal maniac's expression. . . ."

Looking down Bridget shivered and said in a low voice:
" Poor Rivers. . . ."

Luke said pityingly:

" Yes, poor fellow. It's damnable bad luck. But this will be
the last, Bridget! Now we *know*, we'll get him!"

He saw her sway and in two steps he had caught her in his
arms.

She said in a small childlike voice:

" Luke, I'm frightened. . . ."

He said, " It's all over, darling. It's all over. . . ."

She murmured:

" Be kind to me—please. I've been hurt so much."

He said: " We've hurt each other. We won't do that any
more."

CHAPTER SEVENTEEN

Lord Whitfield Talks

DR. THOMAS stared across his consulting-room desk at Luke.

" Remarkable," he said. " Remarkable! You are really
serious, Mr. Fitzwilliam?"

" Absolutely. I am convinced that Ellsworthy is a dangerous
maniac."

" I have not paid special attention to the man. I should say,
though, that he is possibly an abnormal type."

" I'd go a good deal further than that," said Luke grimly.

" You seriously believe that this man Rivers was murdered?"

" I do. You noticed the grains of sand in the wound?"

Dr. Thomas nodded.

" I looked out for them after your statement. I am bound
to say that you were correct."

" That makes it clear, does it not, that the accident was
faked and that the man was killed by a blow from a sandbag
—or at any rate was stunned by one."

" Not necessarily."

" What do you mean?"

Dr. Thomas leaned back and joined his fingertips together.

"Supposing that this man Rivers had been lying out in a
sandpit during the day—there are several about in this part
of the world. That might account for grains of sand in the
hair."

"Man, I tell you he was murdered!"

"You may tell me so," said Dr. Thomas dryly, "but that
doesn't make it a fact."

Luke controlled his exasperation.

"I suppose you don't believe a word of what I'm telling
you."

Dr. Thomas smiled, a kindly superior smile.

"You must admit, Mr. Fitzwilliam, that it's rather a wild
story. You assert that this man Ellsworthy has killed a servant
girl, a small boy, a drunken publican, my own partner and
finally this man Rivers."

"You don't believe it?"

Dr. Thomas shrugged his shoulders.

"I have some knowledge of Humbleby's case. It seems to me
quite out of the question that Ellsworthy could have caused
his death, and I really cannot see that you have any evidence
at all that he did so."

"I don't know how he managed it," confessed Luke, "but
it all hangs together with Miss Pinkerton's story."

"There again you assert that Ellsworthy followed her up
to London and ran her down in a car. Again you haven't a
shadow of proof that happened! It's all—well—romancing!"

Luke said sharply:

"Now that I know where I am it will be my business to
get proofs. I'm going up to London to-morrow to see an old
pal of mine. I saw in the paper two days ago that he's been
made Assistant Commissioner of Police. He knows me and
he'll listen to what I have to say. One thing I'm sure of, he'll
order a thorough investigation of the whole business."

Dr. Thomas stroked his chin thoughtfully.

"Well—no doubt that should be very satisfactory. If it
turns out that you're mistaken——"

Luke interrupted him.

"You definitely don't believe a word of all this?"

"In wholesale murder?" Dr. Thomas raised his eyebrows.

"Quite frankly, Mr. Fitzwilliam, I don't. The thing is too fantastic."

"Fantastic, perhaps. But it hangs together. You've got to admit it hangs together. Once you accept Miss Pinkerton's story as true."

Dr. Thomas was shaking his head. A slight smile came to his lips.

"If you knew some of these old maids as well as I do," he murmured.

Luke rose, trying to control his annoyance.

"At any rate, you're well named," he said. "A doubting Thomas, if there ever was one!"

Thomas replied good-humouredly:

"Give me a few proofs, my dear fellow. That's all I ask. Not just a long melodramatic rigmarole based on what an old lady fancied she saw."

"What old ladies fancy they see is very often right. My Aunt Mildred was positively uncanny! Have you got any aunts yourself, Thomas?"

"Well—er—no."

"A mistake!" said Luke. "Every man should have aunts. They illustrate the triumph of guesswork over logic. It is reserved for aunts to *know* that Mr. A. is a rogue because he looks like a dishonest butler they once had. Other people say reasonably enough that a respectable man like Mr. A. couldn't be a crook. The old ladies are right every time."

Dr. Thomas smiled his superior smile again.

Luke said, his exasperation mounting once more.

"Don't you realise that I'm a policeman myself? I'm not the complete amateur."

Dr. Thomas smiled and murmured:

"In the Mayang Straits!"

"Crime is crime even in the Mayang Straits."

"Of course—of course."

Luke left Dr. Thomas's surgery in a state of suppressed irritation.

He joined Bridget who said:

"Well, how did you get on?"

"He didn't believe me," said Luke. "Which, when you

come to think of it, is hardly surprising. It's a wild story with no proofs. Dr. Thomas is emphatically *not* the sort of man who believes six impossible things before breakfast!"

"Will anybody believe you?"

"Probably not, but when I get hold of old Billy Bones to-morrow, the wheels will start turning. They'll check up on our long-haired friend, Ellsworthy, and in the end they're bound to get somewhere."

Bridget said thoughtfully:

"We're coming out into the open very much, aren't we?"

"We've got to. We can't—we simply can't afford any more murders."

Bridget shivered.

"For God's sake be careful, Luke."

"I'm being careful all right. Don't walk near gates with pine-apples on them, avoid the lonely wood at nightfall, watch out for your food and drink. I know all the ropes."

"It's horrible feeling you're a marked man."

"So long as you're not a marked woman, my sweet."

"Perhaps I am."

"I don't think so. But I don't intend to take risks! I'm watching over you like an old-fashioned guardian angel."

"Is it any good saying anything to the police here?"

Luke considered.

"No, I don't think it is—better go straight to Scotland Yard."

Bridget murmured:

"That's what Miss Pinkerton thought."

"Yes, but *I* shall be watching out for trouble."

Bridget said:

"I know what I'm going to do to-morrow. I shall march Gordon down to that brute's shop and make him buy things."

"Thereby ensuring that our Mr. Ellsworthy is not lying in ambush for me on the steps of Whitehall?"

"That's the idea."

Luke said with some slight embarrassment: "About Whit-field——"

Bridget said quickly:

"Let's leave it till you come back to-morrow. Then we'll have it out."

"Will he be very cut up, do you think?"

"Well——" Bridget considered the question. "He'll be annoyed."

"Annoyed? Ye gods! Isn't that putting it a bit mildly?"

"No. Because you see Gordon doesn't *like* being annoyed! It upsets him!"

Luke said soberly, "I feel rather uncomfortable about it all."

That feeling was uppermost in his mind when he prepared that evening to listen for the twentieth time to Lord Whitfield on the subject of Lord Whitfield. It was, he admitted, a cad's trick to stay in a man's house and steal his fiancée. He still felt, however, that a pot-bellied, pompous, strutting little nincompoop like Lord Whitfield ought never to have aspired to Bridget at all!

But his conscience so far chastened him that he listened with an extra dose of fervent attention and in consequence made a thoroughly favourable impression on his host.

Lord Whitfield was in high good-humour this evening. The death of his erstwhile chauffeur seemed to have exhilarated rather than depressed him.

"Told you that fellow would come to a bad end," he crowed, holding up a glass of port to the light and squinting through it. "Didn't I tell you so yesterday evening?"

"You did, indeed, sir."

"And you see I was right! It's amazing how often I'm right!"

"That must be splendid for you," said Luke.

"I've had a wonderful life—yes, a wonderful life! My path's been smoothed clear before me. I've always had great faith and trust in Providence. That's the secret, Fitzwilliam, that's the secret."

"Yes?"

"I'm a religious man. I believe in good and evil and eternal justice. There *is* such a thing as divine justice, Fitzwilliam, not a doubt of it !"

"I believe in justice, too," said Luke.

Lord Whitfield, as usual, was not interested in the beliefs of other people.

"Do right by your Creator and your Creator will do right

by you! I've always been an upright man. I've subscribed
to charity, and I've made my money honestly. I'm not beholden
to any man! I stand alone. You remember in the Bible how
the patriarchs became prosperous, herds and flocks were added
to them, and their enemies were smitten down!"

Luke stifled a yawn and said:

"Quite—quite."

"It's remarkable—absolutely remarkable," said Lord Whitfield. "The way that a righteous man's enemies are struck
down! Look at yesterday. That fellow abuses me—even goes
so far as to try to raise his hand against me. And what
happens? Where is he to-day?"

He paused rhetorically and then answered himself in an im-
pressive voice:

"Dead! Struck down by divine wrath!"

Opening his eyes a little, Luke said:

"Rather an excessive punishment, perhaps, for a few hasty
words uttered after a glass too much."

Lord Whitfield shook his head.

"It's always like that! Retribution comes swiftly and
terribly. And there's good authentic authority for it. Remember the children that mocked Elisha—how the bears came
out and devoured them. That's the way things happen, Fitzwilliam."

"I always thought that was rather unnecessarily vindictive."

"No, no. You're looking at it the wrong way. Elisha was
a great and holy man. No one could be suffered to mock at
him and live! I understand that because of my own case!"

Luke looked puzzled.

Lord Whitfield lowered his voice.

"I could hardly believe it at first. *But it happened every
time!* My enemies and detractors were cast down and exterminated."

"Exterminated?"

Lord Whitfield nodded gently and sipped his port.

"Time after time. One case quite like Elisha—a little boy.
I came upon him in the gardens here—he was employed by
me then. Do you know what he was doing? He was giving
an imitation of Me—of ME! *Mocking* me! Strutting up and
down with an audience to watch him. Making fun of me on

my own ground! *D'you know what happened to him?* Not
ten days later he fell out of an upper window and was killed!

"Then there was that ruffian Carter—a drunkard and a
man of evil tongue. He came here and abused me. What
happened to him? A week later he was dead—drowned in the
mud. There had been a servant girl, too. She lifted her voice
and called me names. Her punishment soon came. She drank
poison by mistake! I could tell you heaps more. Humbleby
dared to oppose me over the Water scheme. *He* died of blood
poisoning. Oh, it's been going on for years—Mrs. Horton,
for instance, was abominably rude to me and it wasn't long
before *she* passed away."

He paused and leaning forward passed the port decanter
round to Luke.

"Yes," he said. "They all died. Amazing, isn't it?"

Luke stared at him. A monstrous, an incredible suspicion
leapt into his mind! With new eyes, he stared at the small
fat man who sat at the head of the table, who was gently
nodding his head and whose light protuberant eyes met Luke's
with a smiling insouciance.

A rush of disconnected memories flashed rapidly through
Luke's brain. Major Horton saying "Lord Whitfield was very
kind. Sent down grapes and peaches from his hot-house." It
was Lord Whitfield who so graciously allowed Tommy Pierce
to be employed on window-cleaning at the library. Lord Whitfield holding forth on his visit to the Wellerman Kreutz Institute with its serums and germ cultures just a short time before
Dr. Humbleby's death. Everything pointing plainly in one
direction and he, fool that he had been, never even suspecting. . . .

Lord Whitfield was still smiling. A quiet happy smile.
He nodded his head gently at Luke.

"*They all die,*" said Lord Whitfield.

CHAPTER EIGHTEEN

Conference in London

SIR WILLIAM OSSINGTON, known to the cronies of earlier days as Billy Bones, stared incredulously at his friend.

" Didn't you have enough crime out in Mayang?" he asked plaintively. " Have you got to come home and do our work for us here?"

" Crime in Mayang isn't on a wholesale basis," said Luke. " What I'm up against now is a man who's done a round half-dozen murders at least—and got away with it without a breath of suspicion!"

Sir William sighed.

" It does happen. What's his speciality—wives?"

" No, he's not that kind. He doesn't actually think he's God yet—but he soon will."

" Mad?"

" Oh, unquestionably, I should say."

" Ah! but he probably isn't legally mad. There's a difference, you know."

" I should say he knows the nature and consequence of his acts," said Luke.

" Exactly," said Billy Bones.

" Well, don't let's quibble about legal technicalities. We're not nearly at that stage yet. Perhaps we never shall be. What I want from you, old boy, is a few facts. There was a street accident took place on Derby Day between five and six o'clock in the afternoon. Old lady run over in Whitehall and the car didn't stop. Her name was Lavinia Pinkerton. I want you to dig up all facts you can about that."

Sir William sighed. " I can soon get hold of that for you. Twenty minutes ought to do it."

He was as good as his word. In less than that time Luke was talking to the police officer in charge of the matter.

" Yes, sir, I remember the details. I've got most of them

written down here." He indicated the sheet that Luke was studying. "An inquest was held—Mr. Satcherverell was the Coroner. Censure of the driver of the car."

"Did you ever get him?"

"No, sir."

"What make of car was it?"

"It seems pretty certain it was a Rolls—big car driven by a chauffeur. All witnesses unanimous on that point. Most people know a Rolls by sight."

"You didn't get the number?"

"No, unfortunately, nobody thought to look at it. There was a note of a number FZX 4498—but it was the wrong number, a woman spotted it and mentioned it to another woman who gave it to me. I don't know whether the second woman got it wrong but anyway it was no good."

Luke asked sharply: "How did you know it was no good?"

The young officer smiled.

"FZX 4498 is the number of Lord Whitfield's car. That car was standing outside Boomington House at the time in question and the chauffeur was having tea. He had a perfect alibi—no question of his being concerned and the car never left the building till 6.30 when his lordship came out."

"I see," said Luke.

"It's always the way, sir," the man sighed, "half the witnesses have disappeared before a constable can get there and take down particulars."

Sir William nodded.

"We assumed it was probably a number not unlike that FZX 4498—a number beginning probably with two fours. We did our best, but could not trace any car. We investigated several likely numbers but they could all give satisfactory accounts of themselves."

Sir William looked at Luke questioningly.

Luke shook his head. Sir William said:

"Thanks, Bonner, that will do."

When the man had gone out, Billy Bones looked inquiringly at his friend.

"What's it all about, Fitz?"

Luke sighed. "It all tallies. Lavinia Pinkerton was coming up to blow the gaff—to tell the clever people at Scotland Yard

all about the wicked murderer. I don't know whether you'd
have listened to her—probably not——"

"We might," said Sir William. "Things do come through
to us that way. Just hearsay and gossip—we don't neglect
that sort of thing, I assure you."

"That's what the murderer thought. He wasn't going to
risk it. He eliminated Lavinia Pinkerton and although one
woman was sharp enough to spot his number no one believed
her."

Billy Bones sprang upright in his chair.

"You don't mean——"

"Yes, I do. I'll bet you anything you like it was Whitfield
who ran her down. I don't know how he managed it. The
chauffeur was away at tea. Somehow or other, I suppose, he
sneaked away putting on a chauffeur's coat and cap. But he
did it, Billy!"

"Impossible!"

"Not at all. Lord Whitfield has committed at least seven
murders to my certain knowledge and probably a lot more."

"Impossible," said Sir William again.

"My dear fellow, he practically boasted to me of it last
night!"

"He's mad, then?"

"He's mad, all right, but he's a cunning devil. You'll have
to go warily. Don't let him know we suspect him."

Billy Bones murmured: "Incredible . . ."

Luke said: "But true!"

He laid a hand on his friend's shoulder.

"Look here, Billy, old son, we must get right down to this.
Here are the facts."

The two men talked long and earnestly.

On the following day Luke returned to Wychwood. He
drove down early in the morning. He could have returned
the night before but he felt a marked distaste for sleeping
under Lord Whitfield's roof or accepting his hospitality under
the circumstances.

On his way through Wychwood, he drew up his car at
Miss Waynflete's house. The maid who opened the door
stared at him in astonishment but showed him into the little

dining-room where Miss Waynflete was sitting at breakfast.

She rose to receive him in some surprise.

He did not waste time. "I must apologise for breaking in on you at this hour."

He looked round. The maid had left the room, shutting the door. "I'm going to ask you a question, Miss Waynflete. It's rather a personal one, but I think you will forgive me for asking it."

"Please ask me anything you like. I am quite sure your reason for doing so will be a good one."

"Thank you."

He paused.

"I want to know exactly why you broke off your engagement to Lord Whitfield all those years ago?"

She had not expected that. The colour rose in her cheeks and one hand went to her breast.

"Has he told you anything?"

Luke replied: "He told me there was something about a bird—a bird whose neck was wrung . . ."

"He said that?" Her voice was wondering. "He *admitted* it? That's extraordinary!"

"Will you tell me, please."

"Yes, I will tell you. But I beg that you will never speak of the matter to him—to Gordon. It is all past—all over and finished with—I don't want it—raked up."

She looked at him appealingly.

Luke nodded.

"It is only for my personal satisfaction," he said. "I shall not repeat what you tell me."

"Thank you." She had recovered her composure. Her voice was quite steady as she went on. "It was like this. I had a little canary—I was very fond of it—and—perhaps—rather silly about it—girls were, then. They were rather—well—coy about their pets. It must have been irritating to a man—I do realise that."

"Yes," said Luke as she paused.

"Gordon was jealous of the bird. He said one day quite ill-temperedly, 'I believe you prefer that bird to me.' And I, in the rather silly way girls went on in those days, laughed

and held it up on my finger saying something like: ' Of
course I love you, dicky bird, better than a great silly boy!
Of course I do!' Then—oh, it was frightening—Gordon
snatched the bird from me and *wrung its neck.* It was such
a shock—I shall never forget it!"

Her face had gone very pale.

" And so you broke off the engagement?" said Luke.

" Yes. I couldn't feel the same afterwards. You see, Mr.
Fitzwilliam——" she hesitated. " It wasn't just the action
—that *might* have been done in a fit of jealousy and temper
—it was the awful feeling I had *that he'd enjoyed doing it*—
it was *that* that frightened me!"

" Even long ago," murmured Luke. " Even in these
days. . . ."

She laid a hand on his arm.

" Mr. Fitzwilliam——"

He met the frightened appeal in her eyes with a grave
steady look.

" It is Lord Whitfield who committed all these murders!"
he said. " *You've* known that all along, haven't you?"

She shook her head with vigour.

" Not *known* it! If I had *known* it, then—then of course
I would have spoken out—no, it was just a *fear.*"

" And yet you never gave me a hint?"

She clasped her hands in a sudden anguish.

" How could I? How could I? I was fond of him once . . ."

" Yes," said Luke gently. " I see."

She turned away, fumbled in her bag, and a small lace-
edged handkerchief was pressed for a moment to her eyes.
Then she turned back again, dry eyed, dignified and composed.

" I am so glad," she said, " that Bridget has broken off her
engagement. She is going to marry you instead, is she not?"

" Yes."

" That will be much more suitable," said Miss Waynflete
rather primly.

Luke was unable to help smiling a little.

But Miss Waynflete's face grew grave and anxious. She
leaned forward and once more laid a hand on his arm.

" But be very careful," she said. " Both of you must be
very careful."

"You mean—with Lord Whitfield?"

"Yes. It would be better not to tell him."

Luke frowned. "I don't think either of us would like the idea of that."

"Oh! what does that matter? You don't seem to realise that he's *mad—mad*. He won't stand it—not for a moment! If anything happens to her——"

"Nothing shall happen to her!"

"Yes, I know—but *do* realise that you're not a match for him! He's so dreadfully cunning! Take her away at once —it's the only hope. Make her go abroad! You'd better both go abroad!"

Luke said slowly:

"It might be as well if she went. I shall stay."

"I was afraid you would say that. But at any rate *get her away*. *At once*, mind!"

Luke nodded slowly.

"I think," he said, "that you're right."

"I know I'm right! Get her away—*before it's too late.*"

CHAPTER NINETEEN

Broken Engagement

BRIDGET HEARD Luke drive up. She came out on the steps to meet him.

She said without preamble:

"I've told him."

"What?" Luke was taken aback.

His dismay was so patent that Bridget noticed it.

"Luke—what is it? You seem quite upset."

He said slowly:

"I thought we agreed to wait until I came back."

"I know, but I thought it was better to get it over. He was making plans—for our marriage—our honeymoon—all that! I simply *had* to tell him!"

She added—a touch of reproach in her voice:

"It was the only decent thing to do."

He acknowledged it.

"From your point of view, yes. Oh, yes, I see that."

"From every point of view I should have thought!"

Luke said slowly:

"There are times when one can't afford—decency!"

"Luke, what *do* you mean?"

He made an impatient gesture.

"I can't tell you now and here. How did Whitfield take it?"

Bridget said slowly:

"Extraordinarily well. Really extraordinarily well. I felt ashamed. I believe, Luke, that I've under-estimated Gordon —just because he's rather pompous and occasionally futile. I believe really he's rather—well—a great little man!"

Luke nodded.

"Yes, possibly he is a great man—in ways we haven't suspected. Look here, Bridget, you must get out of here as soon as possible."

"Naturally, I shall pack up my things and leave to-day. You might drive me up to town. I suppose we can't both go and stay at the Bells and Motley—that is, if the Ellsworthy contingent have left?"

Luke shook his head.

"No, you'd better go back to London. I'll explain presently. In the meantime I suppose I'd better see Whitfield."

"I suppose it's the thing to do—it's all rather beastly, isn't it? I feel such a rotten little gold digger."

Luke smiled at her.

"It was a fair enough bargain. You'd have played straight with him. Anyway, it's no use lamenting over things that are past and done with! I'll go in and see Whitfield now."

He found Lord Whitfield striding up and down the drawing-room. He was outwardly calm; there was even a slight smile on his lips. But Luke noticed that a pulse in his temple was beating furiously.

He wheeled round as Luke entered.

"Oh! there you are, Fitzwilliam."

Luke said:

"It's no good my saying I'm sorry for what I've done—

that would be hypocritical! I admit that from your point of view I've behaved badly and I've very little to say in defence. These things happen."

Lord Whitfield resumed his pacing.

"Quite—quite!" He waved a hand.

Luke went on.

"Bridget and I have treated you shamefully. But there it is! We care for each other—and there's nothing to be done about it—except tell you the truth and clear out."

Lord Whitfield stopped. He looked at Luke with pale protuberant eyes.

"No," he said, "there's nothing you can do about it!"

There was a very curious tone in his voice. He stood looking at Luke, gently shaking his head as though in commiseration.

Luke said sharply: "What do you mean?"

"There's nothing you can do!" said Lord Whitfield. "It's too late!"

Luke took a step nearer him.

"Tell me what you mean."

Lord Whitfield said unexpectedly:

"Ask Honoria Waynflete. *She*'ll understand. *She* knows what happens. She spoke to me about it once!"

"What does she understand?"

Lord Whitfield said:

"*Evil doesn't go unpunished.* There must be justice! I'm sorry because I'm fond of Bridget. In a way I'm sorry for you both!"

Luke said:

"Are you threatening us?"

Lord Whitfield seemed genuinely shocked.

"No, no, my dear fellow. *I*'ve no feeling in the matter! When I did Bridget the honour to choose her as my wife, she accepted certain responsibilities. Now, she repudiates them —*but there's no going back in this life.* If you break laws you pay the penalty . . ."

Luke clenched both hands. He said:

"You mean that something is going to happen to Bridget? Now understand me, Whitfield, *nothing is going to happen to*

Bridget—nor to me! If you attempt anything of that kind it's the finish. You'd better be careful! I know a good deal about you!"

"It's nothing to do with me," said Lord Whitfield. "I'm only the instrument of a higher Power. What that Power decrees happens!"

"I see you believe that," said Luke.

"Because it's the truth! Any one who goes against me pays the penalty. You and Bridget will be no exception."

Luke said:

"That's where you're wrong. However long a run of luck may be, it breaks in the end. Yours is very near breaking now."

Lord Whitfield said gently:

"My dear young man, you don't know who it is you're talking to. Nothing can touch *Me*!"

"Can't it? We'll see. You'd better watch your step, Whitfield."

A little ripple of movement passed over the other. His voice had changed when he spoke.

"I've been very patient," said Lord Whitfield. "Don't strain my patience too far. Get out of here."

"I'm going," said Luke. "As quick as I can. Remember that I've warned you."

He turned on his heel and went quickly out of the room. He ran upstairs. He found Bridget in her room superintending the packing of her clothes by a housemaid.

"Ready soon?"

"In ten minutes."

Her eyes asked a question which the presence of the maid prevented her from putting into words.

Luke gave a short nod.

He went to his own room and flung his things hurriedly into his suitcase.

He returned ten minutes later to find Bridget ready for departure.

"Shall we go now?"

"I'm ready."

As they descended the staircase they met the butler ascending.

"Miss Waynflete has called to see you, miss."

"Miss Waynflete? Where is she?"

"In the drawing-room with his lordship."

Bridget went straight to the drawing-room, Luke close behind her.

Lord Whitfield was standing by the window talking to Miss Waynflete. He had a knife in his hand—a long slender blade.

"Perfect workmanship," he was saying. "One of my young men brought it back to me from Morocco where he'd been special correspondent. It's Moorish, of course, a Riff knife." He drew a finger lovingly along the blade. What an edge!"

Miss Waynflete said sharply:

"Put it away, Gordon, for goodness' sake!"

He smiled and laid it down among a collection of other weapons on a table.

"I like the feel of it," he said softly.

Miss Waynflete had lost some of her usual poise. She looked white and nervous.

"Ah, there you are, Bridget, my dear," she said.

Lord Whitfield chuckled.

"Yes, there's Bridget. Make the most of her, Honoria. She won't be with us long."

Miss Waynflete said, sharply:

"What d'you mean?"

"Mean? I mean she's going to London. That's right, isn't it? That's all I meant."

He looked round at them all.

"I've got a bit of news for you, Honoria," he said. "Bridget isn't going to marry me after all. She prefers Fitzwilliam here. A queer thing, life. Well, I'll leave you to have your talk."

He went out of the room, his hands jingling the coins in his pockets.

"Oh, dear——" said Miss Waynflete. "Oh, dear——"

The deep distress in her voice was so noticeable that Bridget looked slightly surprised. She said uncomfortably:

"I'm sorry. I really am frightfully sorry."

Miss Waynflete said:

"He's angry—he's frightfully angry—oh, dear, this is terrible. What are we going to do?"

Bridget stared.

"Do? What do you mean?"

Miss Waynflete said, including them both in her reproachful glance:

"You should never have told him!"

Bridget said:

"Nonsense. What else could we do?"

"You shouldn't have told him *now*. You should have waited till you'd got right away."

Bridget said shortly:

"That's a matter of opinion. I think myself it's better to get unpleasant things over as quickly as possible."

"Oh, my dear, if it were only a question of that——"

She stopped. Then her eyes asked a question of Luke.

Luke shook his head. His lips formed the words, "Not yet."

Miss Waynflete murmured, "I see."

Bridget said with some slight exasperation:

"Did you want to see me about something in particular, Miss Waynflete?"

"Well—yes. As a matter of fact I came to suggest that you should come and pay me a little visit. I thought—er—you might find it uncomfortable to remain on here and that you might want a few days to—er—well, mature your plans."

"Thank you, Miss Waynflete, that was very kind of you."

"You see, you'd be quite safe with me and——"

Bridget interrupted:

"*Safe?*"

Miss Waynflete, a little flustered, said hurriedly:

"Comfortable—that's what I meant—quite *comfortable* with me. I mean, not nearly so *luxurious* as here, naturally—but the hot water *is* hot and my little maid Emily really cooks quite nicely."

"Oh, I'm sure everything would be lovely, Miss Waynflete," said Bridget mechanically.

"But, of course, if you are going up to town, that is *much* better. . . ."

Bridget said slowly:

"It's a little awkward. My aunt went off early to a flower show to-day. I haven't had a chance yet to tell her what has happened. I shall leave a note for her telling her I've gone up to the flat."

"You're going to your aunt's flat in London?"

"Yes. There's no one there. But I can go out for meals."

"You'll be alone in that flat? Oh, dear, I shouldn't do that. Not stay there *alone.*"

"Nobody will eat me," said Bridget impatiently. "Besides, my aunt will come up to-morrow."

Miss Waynflete shook her head in a worried manner.

Luke said:

"Better go to a hotel."

Bridget wheeled round on him.

"Why? What's the matter with you all? Why are you treating me as though I was an imbecile child?"

"No, no, dear," protested Miss Waynflete. "We just want you to be *careful*—that's all!"

"But why? Why? What's it all *about*?"

"Look here, Bridget," said Luke. "I want to have a talk with you. But I can't talk here. Come with me now in the car and we'll go somewhere quiet."

He looked at Miss Waynflete.

"May we come to your house in about an hour's time? There are several things I want to say to you."

"Please do. I will wait for you there."

Luke put his hand on Bridget's arm. He gave a nod of thanks to Miss Waynflete.

He said: "We'll pick up the luggage later. Come on."

He led her out of the room and along the hall to the front door. He opened the door of the car. Bridget got in. Luke started the engine and drove rapidly down the drive. He gave a sigh of relief as they emerged from the iron gates.

"Thank God I've got you out of there safely," he said.

"Have you gone quite mad, Luke? Why all this 'hush hush—I can't tell you what I mean now'—business?"

Luke said grimly:

"Well, there are difficulties, you know, in explaining that a man's a murderer when you're actually under his roof!"

CHAPTER TWENTY

We're in it—Together

BRIDGET SAT for a minute motionless beside him. She said:
"*Gordon?*" Luke nodded.

"Gordon? *Gordon—*a *murderer?* Gordon *the* murderer?
I never heard anything so ridiculous in all my life!"

"That's how it strikes you?"

"Yes, indeed. Why, Gordon wouldn't hurt a fly."

Luke said grimly:

"That may be true. I don't know. But he certainly killed
a canary bird, and I'm pretty certain he's killed a large
number of human beings as well."

"My dear Luke, I simply can't believe it!"

"I know," said Luke. "It does sound quite incredible.
Why, he never even entered my head as a possible suspect
until the night before last."

Bridget protested:

"But I know all about Gordon! I know what he's *like*!
He's really a sweet little man—pompous, yes, but rather
pathetic really."

Luke shook his head. "You've got to readjust your ideas
about him, Bridget."

"It's no good, Luke, simply I can't believe it! What put
such an absurd idea into your head? Why, two days ago
you were quite positive it was Ellsworthy."

Luke winced slightly.

"I know. I know. You probably think that to-morrow I
shall suspect Thomas, and the day after I shall be convinced
that it's Horton I'm after! I'm not really so unbalanced as
that. I admit the idea's completely startling when it first
comes to you, but if you look into it a bit closer, you'll see
that it all fits in remarkably well. No wonder Miss Pinkerton
didn't dare to go to the local authorities. *She* knew they'd
laugh at her! Scotland Yard was her only hope."

"But what possible motive could Gordon have for all this killing business? Oh, it's all so *silly* !"

"I know. But don't you realise that Gordon Whitfield has a very exalted opinion of himself?"

Bridget said: "He pretends to be very wonderful and very important. That's just inferiority complex, poor lamb!"

"Possibly that's at the root of the trouble. I don't know. But think, Bridget—just *think* a minute. Remember all the phrases you've used laughingly yourself about him—*lèse-majesté*, etc. Don't you realise that the man's ego is swollen out of all proportion? And it's allied with religion. My dear girl, the man's as mad as a hatter!"

Bridget thought for a minute.

She said at last: "I still can't believe it. What evidence have you got, Luke?"

"Well, there are his own words. He told me, quite plainly and distinctly, the night before last, that anyone who opposed him in any way *always died*."

"Go on."

"I can't quite explain to you what I mean—but it was the way he said it. Quite calm and complacent and—how shall I put it?—quite *used* to the idea! He just sat there smiling to himself. . . . It was uncanny and rather horrible, Bridget!"

"Go on."

"Well, then he went on to give me a list of people who'd passed out because they'd incurred his sovereign displeasure! And, listen to this, Bridget, *the people he mentioned were Mrs. Horton, Amy Gibbs, Tommy Pierce, Harry Carter, Humbleby, and that chauffeur fellow, Rivers.*"

Bridget was shaken at last. She went very pale.

"He mentioned those actual people?"

"Those actual people! *Now* do you believe?"

"Oh, God, I suppose I must. . . . What were his reasons?"

"Horribly trivial—that's what made it so frightening. Mrs. Horton had snubbed him, Tommy Pierce had done imitations of him and made the gardeners laugh, Harry Carter had abused him, Amy Gibbs had been grossly impertinent, Humbleby had dared to oppose him publicly, Rivers threatened him before me and Miss Waynflete——"

Bridget put her hands to her eyes.

"Horrible . . . Quite horrible . . ." she murmured.

"I know. Then there's some other outside evidence. The car that ran down Miss Pinkerton in London was a Rolls, *and its number was the number of Lord Whitfield's car.*"

"That definitely clinches it," said Bridget slowly.

"Yes. The police thought the woman who gave them that number must have made a mistake. Mistake indeed!"

"I can understand that," said Bridget. "When it comes to a rich, powerful man like Lord Whitfield, naturally his story is the one to be believed!"

"Yes. One appreciates Miss Pinkerton's difficulty."

Bridget said thoughtfully:

"Once or twice she said rather queer things to me. As though she were warning me against something. . . . . I didn't understand in the least at the time. . . . I see now!"

"It all fits in," said Luke "That's the way of it. At first one says (as you said), 'Impossible!' and then once one accepts the idea, everything fits in! The grapes he sent to Mrs. Horton—and she thought the nurses were poisoning her! And that visit of his to the Wellerman Kreutz Institute—somehow or other he must have got hold of some culture of germs and infected Humbleby."

"I don't see how he managed that."

"I don't either, *but the connection is there.* One can't get away from that."

"No. . . . As you say, it *fits.* And of course *he* could do things that other people couldn't! I mean he would be so completely above suspicion!"

"I think Miss Waynflete suspected. She mentioned that visit to the institute. Brought it into conversation quite casually—but I believe she hoped I'd act upon it."

"She knew, then, all along?"

"She had a very strong suspicion. I think she was handicapped by having once been in love with him."

Bridget nodded.

"Yes, that accounts for several things. Gordon told me they had once been engaged."

"She wanted, you see, not to believe it was him. But she became more and more sure that it *was.* She tried to give me hints, but she couldn't bear to do anything outright against him! Women are odd creatures! I think, in a way, she still cares about him. . . ."

"Even after he jilted her?"

"*She* jilted *him*. It was rather an ugly story. I'll tell you." He recounted the short, ugly episode. Bridget stared at him.

"Gordon did *that*?"

"Yes. Even in those days, you see, he can't have been normal!"

Bridget shivered and murmured:

"All those years ago . . . all those years. . . ."

Luke said:

"He may have got rid of a lot more people than we shall ever know about! It's just the rapid succession of deaths lately that drew attention to him! As though he'd got reckless with success!"

Bridget nodded. She was silent for a minute or two, thinking, then she asked abruptly:

"What exactly did Miss Pinkerton say to you—in the train that day? How did she begin?"

Luke cast his mind back.

"Told me she was going to Scotland Yard, mentioned the village constable, said he was a nice fellow but not up to dealing with murder."

"That was the first mention of the word?"

"Yes."

"Go on."

"Then she said, '*You're surprised, I can see. I was myself at first. I really couldn't believe it. I thought I must be imagining things.*'"

"And then?"

"I asked her if she was sure she wasn't—imagining things, I mean—and she said quite placidly, '*Oh, no! I might have been the first time, but not the second, or the third or the fourth. After that one knows.*'"

"Marvellous," commented Bridget. "Go on."

"So of course I humoured her—said I was sure she was doing the right thing. I was an unbelieving Thomas if there ever was one!"

"I know. So easy to be wise after the event! I'd have

felt the same, nice and superior to the poor old dame! How did the conversation go on?"

"Let me see—oh! she mentioned the Abercrombie case— you know, the Welsh poisoner. Said she hadn't really believed that there had been a look—a special look—that he gave his victims. But that she believed it now because she had seen it herself."

"What words did she use exactly?"

Luke thought, creasing his brow.

"She said, still in that nice ladylike voice, '*Of course, I didn't really believe that when I read about it—but it's true.*' And I said, 'What's true?' And she said, '*The look on a person's face.*' And by Jove, Bridget, the way she said that absolutely *got* me! Her quiet voice and the look on her face —like someone who had really seen something almost too horrible to speak about!"

"Go on, Luke. Tell me everything."

"And then she enumerated the victims—Amy Gibbs and Carter and Tommy Pierce, and said that Tommy was a horrid boy and Carter drank. And then she said, '*But now—yesterday—it was Dr. Humbleby—and he's such a good man—a really good man.*' And she said if she went to Humbleby and told him, he wouldn't believe her, he'd only laugh!"

Bridget gave a deep sigh.

"I see," she said. "I see."

Luke looked at her.

"What is it, Bridget? What are you thinking of?"

"Something Mrs. Humbleby once said. I wondered—no, never mind, go on. What was it she said to you right at the end?"

Luke repeated the words soberly. They had made an impression on him and he was not likely to forget them.

"I'd said it was difficult to get away with a lot of murders, and she answered, '*No, no, my dear boy, that's where you're wrong. It's very easy to kill—so long as no one suspects you. And you see, the person in question is just the last person any one would suspect. . . .*'"

He was silent. Bridget said with a shiver:

"Easy to kill? Horribly easy—that's true enough! No wonder those words stuck in your mind, Luke. They'll stick in mine—all my life! A man like Gordon Whitfield—oh! of course it's easy."

"It's not so easy to bring it home to him," said Luke.

"Don't you think so? I've an idea I can help there."

"Bridget, I forbid you——"

"You can't. One can't just sit back and play safe. I'm in this, Luke. It may be dangerous—yes, I'll admit that—but I've got to play my part."

"Bridget——"

"I'm *in* this, Luke! I shall accept Miss Waynflete's invitation and stay down here."

"My darling, I implore you——"

"It's dangerous for both of us. I know that. But we're in it, Luke—we're in it—together!"

CHAPTER TWENTY-ONE

" Oh Why Do You Walk Through the Fields in Gloves?"

THE CALM interior of Miss Waynflete's house was almost an anti-climax after that tense moment in the car.

Miss Waynflete received Bridget's acceptance of her invitation a little doubtfully, hastening, however, to reiterate her offer of hospitality by way of showing that her doubts were due to quite another cause than unwillingness to receive the girl.

Luke said:

"I really think it will be the best thing, since you are so kind, Miss Waynflete. I am staying at the Bells and Motley. I'd rather have Bridget under my eye than up in town. After all, remember what happened there before."

Miss Waynflete said:

"You mean—Lavinia Pinkerton?"

"Yes. You would have said, wouldn't you, that any one would be quite safe in the middle of a crowded city."

"You mean," said Miss Waynflete, "that any one's safety depends principally on the fact that nobody wishes to kill them?"

"Exactly. We have come to depend upon what has been called the goodwill of civilisation."

Miss Waynflete nodded her head thoughtfully.

Bridget said:

"How long have you known that—that Gordon was the killer, Miss Waynflete?"

Miss Waynflete sighed.

"That is a difficult question to answer, my dear. I suppose that I have been quite sure, in my inmost heart, for some time. . . . But I did my best not to recognise that belief! You see, I didn't *want* to believe it and so I pretended to myself that it was a wicked and monstrous idea on my part."

Luke said bluntly:

"Have you never been afraid—for yourself?"

Miss Waynflete considered.

"You mean that if Gordon had suspected that I knew, he would have found some means of getting rid of *me*?"

"Yes."

Miss Waynflete said gently:

"I have, of course, been alive to that possibility. . . . I tried to be—careful of myself. But I do not think that Gordon would have considered me a real menace."

"Why?"

Miss Waynflete flushed a little.

"I don't think that Gordon would ever believe that I would do anything to—to bring him into danger."

Luke said abruptly:

"You went as far, didn't you, as to warn him?"

"Yes. That is, I did hint to him that it was odd that any one who displeased him should shortly meet with an accident."

Bridget demanded:

"And what did he say?"

A worried expression passed over Miss Waynflete's face.

"He didn't react at all in the way I meant. He seemed— really it's most extraordinary!—he seemed *pleased*. . . . He said, 'So *you*'ve noticed that?' He quite—quite *preened* himself, if I may use that expression."

"He's mad, of course," said Luke.

Miss Waynflete agreed eagerly.

"Yes, indeed, there isn't any other explanation possible. He's not responsible for his acts." She laid a hand on Luke's arm. "They—they won't *hang* him, will they, Mr. Fitz-william?"

"No, no. Send him to Broadmoor, I expect."

Miss Waynflete sighed and leaned back.

"I'm so glad."

Her eyes rested on Bridget, who was frowning down at the carpet.

Luke said:

"But we're a long way from all that still. I've notified the powers that be and I can say this much, they're prepared to take the matter seriously. But you must realise that we've got remarkably little evidence to go upon."

"We'll get evidence," said Bridget.

Miss Waynflete looked up at her. There was some quality in her expression that reminded Luke of some one or something that he had seen not long ago. He tried to pin down the elusive memory but failed.

Miss Waynflete said doubtfully:

"You are confident, my dear. Well, perhaps you are right."

Luke said:

"I'll go along with the car, Bridget, and fetch your things from the Manor."

Bridget said immediately:

"I'll come too."

"I'd rather you didn't."

"Yes, but I'd rather come."

Luke said irritably:

"Don't do the mother and child act with me, Bridget! I refuse to be protected by you."

Miss Waynflete murmured:

"I really think, Bridget, that it will be quite all right—in a car—and in daylight."

Bridget gave a slightly shamefaced laugh.

"I'm being rather an idiot. This business gets on one's nerves."

Luke said:

"Miss Waynflete protected me home the other night. Come now, Miss Waynflete, admit it! You did, didn't you?"

She admitted it smiling.

"You see, Mr. Fitzwilliam, you were so completely unsuspicious! And if Gordon Whitfield had really grasped the fact that you were down here to look into this business and for no other reason—well, it wasn't very safe. And that's a very lonely lane—*anything* might have happened!"

"Well, I'm alive to the danger now all right," said Luke grimly. "I shan't be caught napping, I can assure you."

Miss Waynflete said anxiously:

"Remember, he is very cunning. And much cleverer than you would ever imagine! Really, a most ingenious mind."

"I'm forewarned."

"Men have courage—one knows that," said Miss Waynflete, "but they are more easily *deceived* than women."

"That's true," said Bridget.

Luke said:

"Seriously, Miss Waynflete, do you really think that I am in any danger? Do you think, in film parlance, that Lord Whitfield is really out to *get* me?"

Miss Waynflete hesitated.

"I think," she said, "that the principal danger is to Bridget. It is *her* rejection of him that is the supreme insult! I think that *after* he has dealt with Bridget he will turn his attention to *you*. But I think that undoubtedly he will try for her *first*."

Luke groaned.

"I wish to goodness you'd go abroad—now—at once, Bridget."

Bridget's lips set themselves together.

"I'm not going."

Miss Waynflete sighed.

"You are a brave creature, Bridget. I admire you."

"You'd do the same in my place."

"Well, perhaps."

Bridget said, her voice dropping to a full, rich note:

"Luke and I are in this together."

She went out with him to the door. Luke said:

"I'll give you a ring from the Bells and Motley when I'm safely out of the lion's den."

"Yes, do."

"My sweet, don't let's get all het up! Even the most accomplished murderers have to have a little time to mature their plans! I should say we're quite all right for a day or two. Superintendent Battle is coming down from London to-day. From then on Whitfield will be under observation."

"In fact, everything is O.K., and we can cut out the melodrama."

Luke said gravely, laying a hand on her shoulder:

"Bridget, my sweet, you will oblige me by not doing anything *rash*!"

"Same to you, darling Luke."

He squeezed her shoulder, jumped into the car and drove off.

Bridget returned to the sitting-room. Miss Waynflete was fussing a little in a gentle spinsterish manner.

"My dear, your room's not *quite* ready yet. Emily is seeing to it. Do you know what I'm going to do? I'm going to get you a nice cup of tea! It's just what you need after all these upsetting incidents."

"It's frightfully kind of you, Miss Waynflete, but I really don't want any."

What Bridget would have liked was a strong cocktail, mainly composed of gin, but she rightly judged that that form of refreshment was not likely to be forthcoming. She disliked tea intensely. It usually gave her indigestion. Miss Waynflete, however, had decided that tea was what her young guest needed. She bustled out of the room and reappeared about five minutes later, her face beaming, carrying a tray on which stood two dainty Dresden cups full of a fragrant, steaming beverage.

"Real Lapsang Souchong," said Miss Waynflete proudly.

Bridget, who disliked China tea even more than Indian, gave a wan smile.

At that moment Emily, a small clumsy-looking girl with pronounced adenoids, appeared in the doorway and said:

"If you please, biss—did you bean the frilled billow-cases?"

Miss Waynflete hurriedly left the room, and Bridget took

advantage of the respite to pour her tea out of the window, narrowly escaping scalding Wonky Pooh, who was on the flower-bed below.

Wonky Pooh accepted her apologies, sprang up on the window-sill and proceeded to wind himself in and out over Bridget's shoulders, purring in an affected manner.

"Handsome!" said Bridget, drawing a hand down his back.

Wonky Pooh arched his tail and purred with redoubled vigour.

"Nice pussy," said Bridget, tickling his ears.

Miss Waynflete returned at that minute.

"Dear me," she exclaimed. "Wonky Pooh has *quite* taken to you, hasn't he? He's so *standoffish* as a rule! Mind his ear, my dear, he's had a bad ear lately and it's still very painful."

The injunction came too late. Bridget's hand had tweaked the painful ear. Wonky Pooh spat at her and retired, a mass of orange offended dignity.

"Oh, dear, has he scratched you?" cried Miss Waynflete.

"Nothing much," said Bridget, sucking a diagonal scratch on the back of her hand.

"Shall I put some iodine on?"

"Oh, no, it's quite all right. Don't let's fuss."

Miss Waynflete seemed a little disappointed. Feeling that she had been ungracious, Bridget said hastily:

"I wonder how long Luke will be?"

"Now don't worry, my dear. I'm sure Mr. Fitzwilliam is well able to look after himself."

"Oh, Luke's tough all right!"

At that moment the telephone rang. Bridget hurried to it. Luke's voice spoke.

"Hallo? That you, Bridget? I'm at the Bells and Motley. Can you wait for your traps till after lunch? Because Battle has arrived here—you know who I mean——"

"The superintendent man from Scotland Yard?"

"Yes. And he wants to have a talk with me right away."

"That's all right by me. Bring my things round after lunch and tell me what he says about it all."

"Right. So long, my sweet."

"So long."

Bridget replaced the receiver and retailed the conversation to Miss Waynflete. Then she yawned. A feeling of fatigue had succeeded her excitement.

Miss Waynflete noticed it.

"You're tired, my dear! You'd better lie down—no, perhaps that would be a bad thing just before lunch. I was just going to take some old clothes to a woman in a cottage not very far away—quite a pretty walk over the fields. Perhaps you'd care to come with me? We'll just have time before lunch."

Bridget agreed willingly.

They went out the back way. Miss Waynflete wore a straw hat and, to Bridget's amusement, had put on gloves.

"We might be going to Bond Street!" she thought to herself.

Miss Waynflete chatted pleasantly of various small village matters as they walked. They went across two fields, crossed a rough lane and then took a path leading through a ragged copse. The day was hot and Bridget found the shade of the trees pleasant.

Miss Waynflete suggested that they should sit down and rest a minute.

"It's really rather oppressively warm to-day, don't you think? I fancy there must be *thunder* about!"

Bridget acquiesced somewhat sleepily. She lay back against the bank—her eyes half-closed—some lines of poetry wandering through her brain.

"*O why do you walk through the fields in gloves O fat white woman whom nobody loves?*"

But that wasn't quite right! Miss Waynflete wasn't fat. She amended the words to fit the case.

"*O why do you walk through the fields in gloves, O lean grey woman whom nobody loves?*"

Miss Waynflete broke in upon her thoughts.

"You're very sleepy, dear, aren't you?"

The words were said in a gentle everyday tone, but something in them jerked Bridget's eyes suddenly open.

Miss Waynflete was leaning forward towards her. Her eyes

were eager, her tongue passed gently over her lips. She repeated her question:

"You're *very* sleepy, aren't you?"

This time there was no mistaking the definite significance of the tone. A flash passed through Bridget's brain—a lightning flash of comprehension, succeeded by one of contempt at her own density!

She had suspected the truth—but it had been no more than a dim suspicion. She had meant, working quietly and secretly, to make sure. But not for one moment had she realised that anything was to be attempted against herself. She had, she thought, concealed her suspicions entirely. Nor would she have dreamed that anything would be contemplated so soon. Fool—seven times fool!

And she thought suddenly:

"The tea—there was something in the tea. *She doesn't know I never drank it.* Now's my chance! I must pretend! What stuff was it, I wonder? Poison? Or just sleeping stuff? She expects me to be sleepy—that's evident."

She let her eyelids droop again. In what she hoped was a natural drowsy voice, she said:

"I do—frightfully. . . . How funny! I don't know when I've felt so sleepy."

Miss Waynflete nodded softly.

Bridget watched the older woman narrowly through her almost closed eyes.

She thought, "I'm a match for her anyway! My muscles are pretty tough—she's a skinny frail old pussy. But I've got to make her *talk*—that's it—make her *talk*!"

Miss Waynflete was smiling. It was not a nice smile. It was sly and not very human.

Bridget thought:

"She's like a goat. God! how like a goat she is! A goat's always been an evil symbol! I see why now! I was right—I was right in that fantastic idea of mine! *Hell hath no fury like a woman scorned.* . . . That was the start of it—it's all there."

She murmured, and this time her voice held a definite note of apprehension.

"I don't know what's the matter with me. . . . I feel so queer—so *very* queer!"

Miss Waynflete gave a swift glance round her. The spot was entirely desolate. It was too far from the village for a shout to be heard. There were no houses or cottages near. She began to fumble with the parcel she carried—the parcel that was supposed to contain old clothes. Apparently it did. The paper came apart, revealing a soft woolly garment. And still those gloved hands fumbled and fumbled.

"*O why do you walk through the fields in gloves?*"

"Yes—why? Why gloves?"

Of course! Of course! The whole thing so beautifully planned!

The wrapping fell aside. Carefully, Miss Waynflete extracted the knife, holding it very carefully so as not to obliterate the fingerprints which were already on it—where the short podgy fingers of Lord Whitfield had held it earlier that day in the drawing-room at Ashe Manor.

The Moorish knife with the sharp blade.

Bridget felt slightly sick. She must play for time—yes and she *must* make the woman talk—this lean, grey woman whom nobody loved. It ought not to be difficult—not really. Because she must want to talk, oh, so badly—and the only person she could ever talk to was some one like Bridget—some one who was going to be silenced for ever.

Bridget said—in a faint, thick voice:

"What's—that—knife?"

And then Miss Waynflete laughed.

It was a horrible laugh, soft and musical and ladylike, and quite inhuman. She said:

"It's for you, Bridget. For you! I've hated you, you know, for a very long time."

Bridget said:

"Because I was going to marry Gordon Whitfield?"

Miss Waynflete nodded.

"You're clever. You're quite clever! This, you see, will be the crowning proof against him. You'll be found here, with your throat cut—and *his* knife, and *his* fingerprints on the knife! Clever the way I asked to see it this morning!

And then I slipped it into my bag wrapped in a handkerchief whilst you were upstairs. So easy! But the whole thing has been easy. I would hardly have believed it."

Bridget said—still in the thick, muffled voice of a person heavily drugged:

" That's—because—you're—so—devilishly—clever . . ."

Miss Waynflete laughed her ladylike little laugh again. She said with a horrible kind of pride:

" Yes, I always had brains, even as a girl! But they wouldn't let me do anything. . . . I had to stay at home—doing nothing. And then Gordon—just a common boot-maker's son, but he had ambition, I knew. I knew he would rise in the world. And he jilted me—jilted *me*! All because of that ridiculous business with the bird."

Her hands made a queer gesture as though she were twisting something.

Again a wave of sickness passed over Bridget.

" Gordon Ragg daring to jilt *me*—Colonel Waynflete's daughter! I swore I'd pay him out for that! I used to think about it night after night. . . . And then we got poorer and poorer. The house had to be sold. *He* bought it! He came along patronising me, offering *me* a job in my own old home. How I hated him then! But I never showed my feelings. We were taught that as girls—a most valuable train-ing. That, I always think, is where breeding tells."

She was silent a minute. Bridget watched her, hardly daring to breathe lest she should stem the flow of words.

Miss Waynflete went on softly:

" All the time I was thinking and thinking. . . . First of all I just thought of killing him. That's when I began to read up criminology—quietly, you know—in the library. And really I found my reading came in most *useful* more than once later. The door of Amy's room, for instance, turning the key in the lock from the outside with pincers after I'd changed the bottles by her bed. How she snored, that girl, quite dis-gusting, it was!"

She paused.

" Let me see, where was I?"

That gift which Bridget had cultivated, which had charmed Lord Whitfield, the gift of the perfect listener, stood her in good stead now. Honoria Waynflete might be a homicidal maniac but she was also something much more common than that. She was a human being who wanted to talk about herself. And with that class of human being Bridget was well fitted to cope.

She said, and her voice had exactly the right invitation in it:

"You meant at first to kill him——"

"Yes, but that didn't satisfy me—much too ordinary—it had to be something better than just killing. And then I got this idea. It just came to me. He should suffer for committing a lot of crimes of which he was quite innocent. He should be a murderer! *He* should be hanged for *my* crimes. Or else they'd say he was mad and he would be shut up all his life. . . . That might be even better."

She giggled now. A horrible little giggle. . . . Her eyes were light and staring with queer elongated pupils.

"As I told you, I read a lot of books on crime. I chose my victims carefully—there was not to be too much suspicion at first. You see," her voice deepened, "I *enjoyed* the killing. . . . That disagreeable woman, Lydia Horton—she'd patronised me—once she referred to me as an 'old maid.' I was glad when Gordon quarrelled with her. Two birds with one stone, I thought! *Such* fun, sitting by her bedside and slipping the arsenic in her tea, and then going out and telling the nurse how Mrs. Horton had complained of the bitter taste of Lord Whitfield's grapes! The stupid woman never repeated that, which was such a pity.

"And then the others! As soon as I heard that Gordon had a grievance against any one, it was *so* easy to arrange for an accident! And he was such a fool—such an incredible fool! I made him believe that there was something very special about him! That any one who went against him suffered. He believed it quite easily. Poor dear Gordon, he'd believe anything. So gullible!"

Bridget thought of herself saying to Luke scornfully:

"Gordon! He could believe anything!"

Easy? How easy! Poor pompous credulous little Gordon. But she must learn more! Easy? This was easy too!] She'd done it as a secretary for years. Quietly encouraged her employers to talk about themselves. And this woman wanted badly to talk, to boast about her own cleverness.

Bridget murmured:

"But how did you manage it all? I don't see how you *could.*"

"Oh, it was *quite* easy! It just needed organisation! When Amy was discharged from the Manor I engaged her at once. I think the hat paint idea was *quite* clever—and the door being locked on the *inside* made *me* quite safe. But of course I was always safe because I never had any *motive*, and you can't expect any one of murder if there isn't a motive. Carter was quite easy too—he was lurching about in the fog and I caught up with him on the footbridge and gave him a quick push. I'm really very strong, you know."

She paused and the soft horrible little giggle came again.

"The whole thing was such *fun*! I shall never forget Tommy's face when I pushed him off the window-sill that day. He hadn't the least idea . . ."

She leaned towards Bridget confidentially.

"People are really very stupid, you know. I'd never realised that before."

Bridget said very softly:

"But then—you're unusually clever."

"Yes—yes—perhaps you're right."

Bridget said:

"Dr. Humbleby—that must have been more difficult?"

"Yes, it was really amazing how that succeeded. It *might* not have worked, of course. But Gordon had been talking to everybody of his visit to the Wellerman Kreutz Institute, and I thought if I *could* manage it so that people remembered that visit and connected it afterwards. And Wonky Pooh's ear was really very nasty, a lot of discharge. I managed to run the point of my scissors into the doctor's hand, and then I was *so* distressed and insisted on putting on a dressing and bandaging it up. He didn't know the dressing had been infected first from Wonky Pooh's ear. Of course, it *mightn't* have worked—it was just a long shot. I was delighted when it did—especially as Wonky Pooh had been Lavinia's cat."

Her face darkened.

"Lavinia Pinkerton! *She* guessed. . . . It was she who

found Tommy that day. And then when Gordon and old Dr.
Humbleby had that row, she caught me looking at Humbleby.
I was off my guard. I was just wondering exactly how I'd do
it. . . . And she knew! I turned round to find her watching
me and—I gave myself away. I saw that she knew. She
couldn't prove anything, of course. I knew that. But I was
afraid all the same some one might believe her. I was afraid
they might believe her at Scotland Yard. I felt sure that was
where she was going that day. I was in the same train and I
followed her.

"The whole thing was so easy. She was on an island crossing Whitehall. I was close behind her. She never saw me.
A big car came along and I shoved with all my might. I'm
very strong! She went right down in front of it. I told the
woman next to me I'd seen the number of the car and gave
her the number of Gordon's Rolls. I hoped she'd repeat it to
the police.

"It was lucky the car didn't stop. Some chauffeur joy-
riding without his master's knowledge, I suspect. Yes, I was
lucky there. I'm always lucky. That scene the other day with
Rivers, and Luke Fitzwilliam as witness. I've had such fun
leading him along! Odd how difficult it was to make him
suspect Gordon. But after Rivers's death he would be sure to
do so. He must!

"And now—well, this will just finish the whole thing
nicely."

She got up and came towards Bridget. She said softly:

"Gordon jilted me! He was going to marry you. All my
life I've been disappointed. I've had nothing—nothing at
all. . . ."

"*O lean grey woman whom nobody loves. . . .*"

She was bending over her, smiling, with mad light eyes.
. . . The knife gleamed. . . .

With all her youth and strength, Bridget sprang. Like a
tiger-cat, she flung herself full force on the other woman,
knocking her back, seizing her right wrist.

Taken by surprise, Honoria Waynflete fell back before
the onslaught. But then, after a moment's inertia, she began
to fight. In strength there was no comparison between them.
Bridget was young and healthy with muscles toughened by

games. Honoria Waynflete was a slender-built, frail creature.

But there was one factor on which Bridget had not reckoned. *Honoria Waynflete was mad.* Her strength was the strength of the insane. She fought like a devil and her insane strength was stronger than the sane muscled strength of Bridget. They swayed to and fro, and still Bridget strove to wrest the knife away from her, and still Honoria Waynflete hung on to it.

And then, little by little, the mad woman's strength began to prevail. Bridget cried out now:

"*Luke ... Help ... Help....*"

But she had no hope of help coming. She and Honoria Waynflete were alone. Alone in a dead world. With a supreme effort she wrenched the other's wrist back, and at last she heard the knife fall.

The next minute Honoria Waynflete's two hands had fastened round her neck in a maniac grasp, squeezing the life out of her. She gave one last choked cry. . . .

CHAPTER TWENTY-TWO

Mrs. Humbleby Speaks

LUKE WAS favourably impressed by the appearance of Superintendent Battle. He was a solid, comfortable-looking man with a broad red face and a large handsome moustache. He did not exactly express brilliance at a first glance, but a second glance was apt to make an observant person thoughtful, for Superintendent Battle's eye was unusually shrewd.

Luke did not make the mistake of underestimating him. He had met men of Battle's type before. He knew that they could be trusted, and that they invariably got results. He could not have wished for a better man to be put in charge of the case.

When they were alone together Luke said:

"You're rather a big noise to be sent down on a case like this?"

Superintendent Battle smiled.

"It may turn out to be a serious business, Mr. Fitzwilliam. When a man like Lord Whitfield is concerned, we don't want to have any mistakes."

"I appreciate that. Are you alone?"

"Oh, no. Got a detective-sergeant with me. He's at the other pub, the Seven Stars, and his job is to keep an eye on his lordship."

"I see."

Battle asked:

"In your opinion, Mr. Fitzwilliam, there's no doubt whatever? You're pretty sure of your man?"

"On the facts I don't see that any alternative theory is possible. Do you want me to give you the facts?"

"I've had them, thank you, from Sir William."

"Well, what do *you* think? I suppose it seems to you wildly unlikely that a man in Lord Whitfield's position should be a homicidal criminal?"

"Very few things seem unlikely to me," said Superintendent Battle. "Nothing's impossible in crime. That's what I've always said. If you were to tell me that a dear old maiden lady, or an archbishop, or a schoolgirl, was a dangerous criminal, I wouldn't say no. I'd look into the matter."

"If you've heard the main facts of the case from Sir William, I'll just tell you what happened this morning," said Luke.

He ran over briefly the main lines of his scene with Lord Whitfield. Superintendent Battle listened with a good deal of interest.

He said:

"You say he was fingering a knife. Did he make a special point of that knife, Mr. Fitzwilliam? Was he threatening with it?"

"Not openly. He tested the edge in a rather nasty way— a kind of æsthetic pleasure about that that I didn't care about. Miss Waynflete felt the same, I believe."

"That's the lady you spoke about—the one who's known Lord Whitfield all her life, and was once engaged to marry him?"

"That's right."

Superintendent Battle said:

"I think you can make your mind easy about the young lady, Mr. Fitzwilliam. I'll have some one put on to keep a sharp watch on her. With that, and with Jackson tailing his lordship, there ought to be no danger of anything happening."

"You relieve my mind a good deal," said Luke.

The superintendent nodded sympathetically.

"It's a nasty position for you, Mr. Fitzwilliam. Worrying about Miss Conway. Mind you, I don't expect this will be an easy case. Lord Whitfield must be a pretty shrewd man. He will probably lie low for a good long while. That is, unless he's got to the last stage."

"What do you call the last stage?"

"A kind of swollen egoism where a criminal thinks he simply can't be found out! He's too clever and everybody else is too stupid! Then, of course, we get him!"

Luke nodded. He rose.

"Well," he said, "I wish you luck. Let me help in any way I can."

"Certainly."

"There's nothing that you can suggest?"

Battle turned the question over in his mind.

"I don't think so. Not at the moment. I just want to get the general hang of things in the place. Perhaps I could have another word with you in the evening?"

"Rather."

"I shall know better where we are then."

Luke felt vaguely comforted and soothed. Many people had had that feeling after an interview with Superintendent Battle.

He glanced at his watch. Should he go round and see Bridget before lunch?

Better not, he thought. Miss Waynflete might feel that she had to ask him to stay for the meal, and it might disorganise her housekeeping. Middle-aged ladies, Luke knew from experience with aunts, were liable to be fussed over problems of housekeeping. He wondered if Miss Waynflete was an aunt? Probably.

He had strolled out to the door of the inn. A figure in black hurrying down the street stopped suddenly when she saw him.

" Mr. Fitzwilliam."

" Mrs. Humbleby."

He came forward and shook hands.

She said:

" I thought you had left?"

" No—only changed my quarters. I'm staying here now."

" And Bridget? I heard she had left Ashe Manor?"

" Yes, she has."

Mrs. Humbleby sighed.

" I am so glad—so very glad she has gone right away from Wychwood."

" Oh, she's still here. As a matter of fact, she's staying with Miss Waynflete."

Mrs. Humbleby moved back a step. Her face, Luke noted with surprise, looked extraordinarily distressed.

" Staying with Honoria Waynflete? Oh, but *why*?"

" Miss Waynflete very kindly asked her to stay for a few days."

Mrs. Humbleby gave a little shiver. She came close to Luke and laid a hand on his arm.

" Mr. Fitzwilliam, I know I have no right to say anything— anything at all. I have had a lot of sorrow and grief lately and—perhaps—it makes me fanciful! These feelings of mine may be only sick fancies."

Luke said gently:

" What feelings?"

" This conviction I have of—of *evil*!"

She looked timidly at Luke. Seeing that he merely bowed his head gravely and did not appear to question her statement, she went on:

" *So much wickedness*—that is the thought that is always with me—wickedness here in Wychwood. And that woman is at the bottom of it all. I am sure of it!"

Luke was mystified.

" What woman?"

Mrs. Humbleby said:

" Honoria Waynflete is, I am sure, a very wicked woman! Oh, I see, you don't believe me! No one believed Lavinia Pinkerton either. *But we both felt it.* She, I think, knew more than I did. . . . Remember, Mr. Fitzwilliam, if a woman is not happy she is capable of terrible things."

Luke said gently:

"That may be—yes."

Mrs. Humbleby said quickly:

"You don't believe me? Well, why should you? But I can't forget the day when John came home with his hand bound up from her house, though he pooh-poohed it and said it was only a scratch."

She turned.

"Good-bye. Please forget what I have just said. I—I don't feel quite myself these days."

Luke watched her go. He wondered why Mrs. Humbleby called Honoria Waynflete a wicked woman. Had Dr. Humbleby and Honoria Waynflete been friends, and was the doctor's wife jealous?

What had she said? "Nobody believed Lavinia Pinkerton either." Then Lavinia Pinkerton must have confided some of her suspicions to Mrs. Humbleby.

With a rush the memory of the railway carriage came back, and the worried face of a nice old lady. He heard again an earnest voice saying, "*The look on a person's face.*" And the way her own face had changed as though she were seeing something very clearly in her mind. Just for a moment, he thought, her face had been quite different, the lips drawn back from the teeth and a queer, almost gloating look in her eyes.

He suddenly thought: *But I've seen some one look just like that—that same expression. . . . Quite lately—when?* This morning! Of course! Miss Waynflete, when she was looking at Bridget in the drawing-room at the Manor.

And quite suddenly another memory assailed him. One of many years ago. His Aunt Mildred saying, "She looked, you know, my dear, quite *half-witted*!" and just for a minute her own sane comfortable face had borne an imbecile, mindless expression. . . .

Lavinia Pinkerton had been speaking of the look she had seen on a man's—no, a *person's* face. Was it possible that, just for a second, her vivid imagination had *reproduced the look that she saw—the look of a murderer looking at his next victim. . . .*

Half unaware of what he was doing, Luke quickened his pace towards Miss Waynflete's house.

A voice in his brain was saying over and over again:

"Not a *man*—she never mentioned a *man*—*you* assumed it was a man because you were thinking of a man—but *she* never said so. . . . Oh, God, am I quite mad? It isn't possible what I'm thinking . . . surely it isn't *possible*—it wouldn't make sense. . . . But I *must* get to Bridget. I *must* know she's all right. . . . Those eyes—those queer, light amber eyes. Oh, I'm mad! I must be mad! Whitfield's the criminal! He *must* be. He practically *said* so!"

And still, like a nightmare, he saw Miss Pinkerton's face in its momentary impersonation of something horrible and not quite sane.

The stunted little maid opened the door to him. A little startled by his vehemence, she said:

"The lady's gone out. Miss Waynflete told me so. I'll see if Miss Waynflete's in."

He pushed past her, went into the drawing-room. Emily ran upstairs. She came down breathless.

"The mistress is out too."

Luke took her by the shoulder.

"Which way? Where did they go?"

She gaped at him.

"They must have gone out by the back. I'd have seen them if they'd gone out frontways because the kitchen looks out there."

She followed him as he raced out through the door into the tiny garden and out beyond. There was a man clipping a hedge. Luke went up to him and asked a question, striving to keep his voice normal.

The man said slowly:

"Two ladies? Yes. Some while since. I was having my dinner under the hedge. Reckon they didn't notice me."

"*Which way did they go?*"

He strove desperately to make his voice normal. Yet the other's eyes opened a little wider as he replied slowly:

"Across them fields. . . . Over that way. I don't know where after that."

Luke thanked him and began to run. His strong feeling of urgency was deepened. He *must* catch up with them—he *must*! He might be quite mad. In all probability they were just taking an amicable stroll, but something in him clamoured for haste. More haste!

He crossed the two fields, stood hesitating in a country lane. Which way now?

And then he heard the call—faint, far away, but unmistakable. . . .

"*Luke. Help.*" And again, "*Luke . .*"

Unerringly he plunged into the wood and ran in the direction from which the cry had come There were more sounds now—scuffling—panting—a low gurgling cry.

He came through the trees in time to tear a mad woman's hands from her victim's throat, to hold her, struggling, foaming, cursing, till at last she gave a convulsive shudder and turned rigid in his grasp.

CHAPTER TWENTY-THREE

New Beginning

"BUT I don't understand," said Lord Whitfield. "I don't understand."

He strove to maintain his dignity, but beneath the pompous exterior a rather pitiable bewilderment was evident. He could hardly credit the extraordinary things that were being told him.

"It's like this, Lord Whitfield," said Battle patiently. "To begin with there is a touch of insanity in the family. We've found that out now. Often the way with these old families. I should say she had a predisposition that way. And then she was an ambitious lady—and she was thwarted. First her career and then her love affair." He coughed. "I understand it was *you* who jilted *her*?"

Lord Whitfield said stiffly:

" I don't like the term jilt."

Superintendent Battle amended the phrase.

" It was you who terminated the engagement?"

" Well—yes."

" Tell us why, Gordon," said Bridget.

Lord Whitfield got rather red. He said:

" Oh, very well, if I must. Honoria had a canary. She was very fond of it. It used to take sugar from her lips. One day it pecked her violently instead. She was angry and picked it up—and—wrung its neck! I—I couldn't feel the same after that. I told her I thought we'd both made a mistake."

Battle nodded. He said:

" That was the beginning of it! As she told Miss Conway, she turned her thoughts and her undoubted mental ability to one aim and purpose."

Lord Whitfield said incredulously:

" To get *me* convicted as a murderer? I can't believe it."

Bridget said, " It's true, Gordon. You know, you were surprised yourself at the extraordinary way that everybody who annoyed you was instantly struck down."

" There was a reason for that."

" Honoria Waynflete was the reason," said Bridget. " Do get it into your head, Gordon, that it wasn't Providence that pushed Tommy Pierce out of the window, and all the rest of them. It was Honoria."

Lord Whitfield shook his head.

" It all seems to me quite incredible!" he said.

Battle said:

" You say you got a telephone message this morning?"

" Yes—about twelve o'clock. I was asked to go to the Shaw Wood at once as you, Bridget, had something to say to me. I was not to come by car but to walk."

Battle nodded.

" Exactly. That would have been the finish. Miss Conway would have been found with her throat cut; and beside her *your* knife with *your* fingerprints on it! *And* you yourself would have been seen in the vicinity at the time! You wouldn't have had a leg to stand upon. Any jury in the world would have convicted you."

"Me?" said Lord Whitfield, startled and distressed. "Any one would have believed a thing like that of Me?"

Bridget said gently:

"I didn't, Gordon. I never believed it."

Lord Whitfield looked at her coldly, then he said stiffly:

"In view of my character and my standing in the county, I do not believe that any one for one moment would have believed in such a monstrous charge!"

He went out with dignity and closed the door behind him. Luke said:

"He'll never realise that he was really in danger!"

Then he said:

"Go on, Bridget, tell me how you came to suspect the Waynflete woman."

Bridget explained.

"It was when you were telling me that Gordon was the killer. I couldn't believe it! You seee, I knew him so *well*. I'd been his secretary for two years! I knew him in and out! I knew that he was pompous and petty and completely self-absorbed, but I knew, too, that he was a kindly person and almost absurdly tender-hearted. It worried him even to kill a wasp. That story about his killing Miss Waynflete's canary —it was all *wrong*. He just couldn't have done it. He'd told me once that he had jilted her. Now you insisted that it was *the other way about*. Well, that *might* be so! His pride might not have allowed him to admit that she had thrown him over. But not the canary story! That simply wasn't Gordon! He didn't even shoot because seeing things killed made him feel sick.

"So I simply knew that that part of the story was untrue. But if so, *Miss Waynflete must have lied*. And it was really, when you came to think of it, *a very extraordinary lie*! And I wondered suddenly if she'd told any more lies. She was a very proud woman—one could see that. To be thrown over must have hurt her pride horribly. It would probably make her feel very angry and revengeful against Lord Whitfield— especially, I felt, if he turned up again later all rich and prosperous and successful. I thought, 'Yes, she'd probably enjoy helping to fix a crime upon him.' And then a curious sort of whirling feeling came in my brain and I thought—

but suppose *everything* she says is a lie—and I suddenly saw how easily a woman like that could make a fool of a man! And I thought, 'It's fantastic, but suppose it was *she* who killed all these people and fed Gordon up with the idea that it was a kind of divine retribution!' It would be quite easy for her to make him believe that. As I told you once, Gordon would believe anything! And I thought, '*Could* she have done all those murders?' And I saw that she could! She could give a shove to a drunken man—and push a boy out of a window, and Amy Gibbs had died in her house. Mrs. Horton, too—Honoria Waynflete used to go and sit with her when she was ill. Dr. Humbleby was more difficult. I didn't know then that Wonky Pooh had a nasty septic ear and that she infected the dressing she put on his hand. Miss Pinkerton's death was even more difficult, because I couldn't imagine Miss Waynflete dressed up as a chauffeur driving a Rolls.

"And then, suddenly, I saw that that was the easiest of the lot! It was the old shove from behind—easily done in a crowd. The car didn't stop and she saw a fresh opportunity and told another woman she had seen the number of the car, and gave the number of Lord Whitfield's Rolls.

"Of course, all this only came very confusedly through my head. But if Gordon definitely *hadn't* done the murders—and I knew—yes, *knew* that he hadn't—well, who *had*? And the answer seemed quite clear. '*Someone who hates Gordon!*' Who hates Gordon? Honoria Waynflete, of course.

"And then I remembered that Miss Pinkerton had definitely spoken of a *man* as the killer. That knocked out all my beautiful theory, because, unless Miss Pinkerton was *right*, *she wouldn't have been killed.* . . . So I got you to repeat exactly Miss Pinkerton's words and I soon discovered that she hadn't actually said '*Man*' once. Then I felt that I was definitely on the right track! I decided to accept Miss Waynflete's invitation to stay with her and I resolved to try to ferret out the truth."

"Without saying a word to me?" said Luke angrily.

"But, my sweet, you were so *sure*—and I wasn't sure a bit! It was all vague and doubtful. But I never dreamed that I was in any danger. I thought I'd have plenty of time . . ."

She shivered.

"Oh, Luke, it was horrible. . . . Her eyes. . . . And that dreadful, polite, inhuman laugh. . . ."

Luke said with a slight shiver: "I shan't forget how I only got there just in time."

He turned to Battle. "What's she like now?"

"Gone right over the edge," said Battle. "They do, you know. They can't face the shock of not having been as clever as they thought they were."

Luke said ruefully:

"Well, I'm not much of a policeman! I never suspected Honoria Waynflete once. You'd have done better, Battle."

"Maybe, sir, maybe not. You'll remember my saying that nothing's impossible in crime. I mentioned a maiden lady, I believe."

"You also mentioned an archbishop and a schoolgirl! Am I to understand that you consider all these people as potential criminals?"

Battle's smile broadened to a grin.

"Any one may be a criminal, sir, that's what I meant."

"Except Gordon," said Bridget. "Luke, let's go and find him."

They found Lord Whitfield in his study busily making notes.

"Gordon," said Bridget in a small meek voice. "Please, now that you know everything, will you forgive us?"

Lord Whitfield looked at her graciously.

"Certainly, my dear, certainly. I realise the truth. I was a busy man. I neglected you. The truth of the matter is as Kipling so wisely puts it: 'He travels the fastest who travels alone.' My path in life is a lonely one." He squared his shoulders. "I carry a big responsibility. I must carry it alone. For me there can be no companionship, no easing of the burden—I must go through life alone—till I drop by the wayside."

Bridget said:

"Dear Gordon! You really are sweet!"

Lord Whitfield frowned.

"It is not a question of being sweet. Let us forget all this nonsense. I am a busy man."

" I know you are."

" I am arranging for a series of articles to start at once. Crimes committed by Women through the Ages."

Bridget gazed at him with admiration.

" Gordon, I think that's a wonderful idea."

Lord Whitfield puffed out his chest.

" So please leave me now. I must not be disturbed. I have a lot of work to get through."

Luke and Bridget tiptoed from the room.

" But he really *is* sweet ! " said Bridget.

" Bridget, I believe you were really fond of that man !,"

" Do you know, Luke, I believe I was."

Luke looked out of the window.

" I'll be glad to get away from Wychwood. I don't like this place. There's a lot of wickedness here, as Mrs. Humbleby would say. I don't like the way Ashe Ridge broods over the village."

" Talking of Ashe Ridge, what about Ellsworthy?"

Luke laughed a little shamefacedly.

" That blood on his hands?"

" Yes."

" They'd sacrificed a white cock apparently !"

" How perfectly disgusting !"

" I think something unpleasant is going to happen to our Mr. Ellsworthy. Battle is planning a little surprise."

Bridget said:

" And poor Major Horton never even attempted to kill his wife, and Mr. Abbot, I suppose, just had a compromising letter from a lady, and Dr. Thomas is just a nice unassuming young doctor."

" He's a superior ass ! "

" You say that because you're jealous of his marrying Rose Humbleby."

" She's much too good for him."

" I always have felt you liked that girl better than me ! "

" Darling, aren't you being rather absurd?"

" No, not really."

She was silent a minute and then said:

" Luke, do you like me now?"

He made a movement towards her but she warded him off.

"I said *like,* Luke—not *love.*"

"Oh! I see. . . . Yes, I do. . . I *like* you, Bridget, as well as loving you."

Bridget said: "I like you, Luke. . . ."

They smiled at each other—a little timidly—like children who have made friends at a party.

Bridget said:

"Liking is more important than loving. It lasts. I want what is between us to last, Luke. I don't want us just to love each other and marry and get tired of each other and then want to marry some one else."

"Oh! my dear Love, I know. You want reality. So do I. What's between us will last for ever because it's founded on reality."

"Is that true, Luke?"

"It's true, my sweet. That's why, I think, I was afraid of loving you."

"I was afraid of loving you, too."

"Are you afraid now?"

"No."

He said:

"We've been close to Death for a long time. Now—that's over! Now—we'll begin to Live. . . ."

THE END

Agatha Christie
The Murder on the Links 60p

'One can see by his face that he was stabbed in the back,'
said Poirot.

But the strangest feature of the case was where they found
the body – in an open grave!

Poirot Investigates 60p

In a shooting-box on the bleak Derbyshire moors a man is
killed, and Poirot solves the crime – 150 miles away!

The Hollow 60p

'It strikes me, M. Poirot, that taking it all round you're far
and away the most suspicious character in the case!'

They Came to Baghdad 60p

Victoria Jones does not agree with office life – nor it with
her . . . Unemployed yet again, she chances on an
opportunity to fly to Baghdad.

A job with a mysterious organization, three words uttered
by a dying man, and Victoria is caught in the relentless coil
of international intrigue . . .

4.50 from Paddington 60p

Nobody believed Mrs McGillicuddy when she reported
having seen a woman being strangled in a first-class carriage
of a train running parallel to her own.

Lionel Black
The Life and Death of Peter Wade 50p

What secret lies in the life story of a second-rate actor? A secret that must be suppressed – by murder if necessary.

Why was the glamorous pop-star wife so anxious for her husband's peccadilloes to be revealed?

How can the actor's past influence the struggle for power in an emergent African state?

Finding the answers led Johnny Trott, obscure journalist, from the frying pan into some very hot fires . . .

Ransom for a Nude 50p

Why and how would anyone steal a famous Velasquez nude the night before it is due to be auctioned? Who would dare buy the painting?

A pretty deb and an ex-actor share their audacious plan with a cold-blooded mercenary – and the scene is set for an ingenious crime, planned with a ruthlessness that does not exclude murder!

You can buy these and other Pan books from booksellers and
newsagents; or direct from the following address:
Pan Books, Cavaye Place, London SW10 9PG
Send purchase price plus 15p for the first book and 5p for
each additional book, to allow for postage and packing
Prices quoted are applicable in UK

While every effort is made to keep prices low, it is sometimes
necessary to increase prices at short notice. Pan Books reserve the
right to show on covers new retail prices which may differ
from those advertised in the text or elsewhere